9/08(11)(circled)(illegible)4/08

IN SUNSHINE AND IN SHADOW

For Nicola, her summer vacation job — looking after an adorable little boy named Carlo — is a dream come true. But with the growing fear of kidnap, the dream is becoming a nightmare. Both Carlo's grandfather and his father, Angelo (who is working undercover for the Carabinieri) are widowers. Amidst the summer crowds on the Amalfi Coast, it is Nicola's job to keep their beloved child safe. She will do it if it kills her. But she must on no account fall in love with the disturbingly attractive Angelo.

Books by Ravey Sillars
in the Linford Romance Library:

THEIR ISLAND OF DREAMS
HIS BROTHER'S KEEPER
RETURN TO TORQUILLAN

RAVEY SILLARS

IN SUNSHINE AND IN SHADOW

Complete and Unabridged

LINFORD
Leicester

First published in Great Britain in 1997

First Linford Edition
published 2005

British Library CIP Data

Sillars, Ravey
    In sunshine and in shadow.—Large print ed.—
    Linford romance library
    1. Love stories
    2. Large type books
    I. Title
    823.9'14 [F]

    ISBN 1–84395–861–9

Published by
F. A. Thorpe (Publishing)
Anstey, Leicestershire

Set by Words & Graphics Ltd.
Anstey, Leicestershire
Printed and bound in Great Britain by
T. J. International Ltd., Padstow, Cornwall

This book is printed on acid-free paper

Off To Italy!

'Now, remember, Nicola, if you discover you don't like living over there, or if you can't get along with the Ranieris, you've just to come home.'

'Oh, Mum!' Nicola Gray tried to stifle her exasperation. 'I wish you would stop treating me like a child!'

Linda smiled in spite of herself. Nicola had just turned twenty — so mature in her own eyes, yet still so vulnerable in her mother's.

Nicola caught her mother's expression and went on in a gentler tone.

'Don't worry, Mum, nothing will go wrong. I'll be back safe and sound at the end of August.'

'That's three whole months away!' Fraser Blyth, Nicola's boyfriend, muttered glumly. 'I just wish I could have landed a summer job out there beside you!'

1

'Me, too,' Nicola said wistfully and looked up at the young man standing beside her.

Leaving Fraser behind was the one cloud on her otherwise bright blue horizon. She would miss him very much indeed.

Linda studied him with very different feelings. Perhaps it was his appearance that made her wary of him. His black leather jacket was liberally embellished with silver studs and chains, and the narrow leather trousers, disappearing into heavy boots, added to the impression of height and power about him.

Although his eyes were a harmless blue and could be kind, his fair hair was tied back with a black shoelace into a ponytail, a style that didn't appeal to Linda.

But most of all she worried about the powerful motorcycle he roared around on. When he took Nicola out at night Linda could never get to sleep until she heard the bike return safely.

A feeling of quiet desperation swept

2

over her now as she glanced about the airport lounge, as if seeking some way to prevent her child from leaving.

Instead, she forced a smile. She mustn't spoil Nicola's departure by letting her own apprehension show. After all, her fears had no foundation.

'Just don't speak to any strange men,' Fraser advised Nicola, only half joking.

'I won't,' she promised. And then she laughed. 'Honestly, it's like being seen off by a pair of mother hens! How many times do I have to tell you — I'll be all right! I don't need anyone to keep an eye on me. Italians are lovely. Think of Grandpa! He was Italian and he was the most charming man I've ever known.'

'Me, too.' Linda had very fond memories of her father from whom she'd learned so much. Then she smiled at her daughter, who seemed totally unaware that she herself had inherited much of his charm, together with a distinctly Italian appearance.

'It's the Italian charm that worries

me,' Fraser said. 'I'm scared you'll be swept off your feet by a handsome Latin and forget all about me!'

'Don't worry.' Nicola twinkled up at him. 'There's no danger of that. I'll be too busy missing you.'

Personally Linda thought it might not be a bad thing if Nicola should become interested in some other young men. Fraser Blyth seemed to be far too significant in her life at present and Linda wasn't sure that he was the best influence on her.

Nicola had met him during her first year at university. The following year Fraser had dropped out, saying loftily that he would learn more in 'the school of life'. The romance, however, had endured, and according to Nicola a year of low-paid, dead-end work had changed Fraser's views. Now he was hoping to do a college course that would help him get a better job.

Just then, Linda's attention was caught by some acquaintances greeting her, and as she turned away to speak to

4

them Fraser seized Nicola's hand and squeezed it tightly.

'I don't want you to go.' He gazed down into her entrancing face, hopelessly aware of how much he was going to miss her. 'I can't bear the thought of not seeing you for three months. Maybe I could come over on the bike sometime?'

'Oh, Fraser, this is tearing me apart, too — please don't make it any worse! And you know it's too far for you to travel.'

The young couple clung together, their hearts too full to say more, until the announcements came for the passengers of Nicola's flight to proceed to the departure lounge.

Linda hurried back to be by her daughter's side and in the flurry of last-minute embraces and Linda's reminders to take care, Fraser only managed to kiss Nicola again briefly.

'I'm not much of a letter-writer — but you'll hear from me,' he said earnestly. 'I'll be in touch soon, I promise!'

5

It was with an aching heart that Linda stood with Fraser, watching Nicola walk away. The girl turned once to wave before she disappeared and the light around them seemed to dim.

★ ★ ★

As she drove Fraser back to Fieldbridge, Linda tried to make light conversation to stifle the ache in her heart.

'Nicola never forgot her grandfather's stories,' she said. 'She's been determined to visit Italy ever since she was tiny. This is her dream coming true.'

Fraser nodded. 'Nanny to a four-year-old boy. It'll improve her Italian, though.'

'Oh, yes — children are such chatterboxes. And of course, there's Giorgio Ranieri, the child's grandfather. He's a widower, isn't he? Nicola and the little boy should enjoy staying with him for the summer.'

'I hope he doesn't fancy Nicola!'

6

Fraser commented grimly.

'Don't be silly, Fraser!' The idea both amused and horrified Linda. 'He's old enough to be her father!'

In spite of herself, those words brought a lump to her throat, for Nicola's own father had died four years ago.

Stifling a sigh, she began again brightly: 'Anyway, I was telling you about Nicola's grandfather. You know, he always wanted to take us all back to where he came from, a little village high above the Amalfi coast. But he died before he could manage it.

'Mum used to try to persuade him to go alone — but he said he only wanted to go in order to show off his beautiful wife and his two children, me and my brother, Paul.' Linda slowed for some traffic lights. 'He kept in touch by letter, of course.'

'Your mum sounds quite a character herself, though,' Fraser said. 'Nicola's told me a lot about her.'

Linda laughed. 'She certainly is!

7

She's still very independent — too much so at times! You never know what she's going to get involved in next. It's just as well she lives not too far away. It lets me keep an eye on her.'

The lights changed and she pulled away from the crossing.

'Do you want me to drop you off at the supermarket?' she asked, glancing at him.

'Yes, please,' he replied. 'It's about time for my shift to start.'

'How's the work going?'

'Fine, I suppose.' It was Fraser's turn to sigh. 'I'm mainly unpacking and stacking. It doesn't exactly overtax the brain!'

'A bit boring?' she guessed.

He shrugged. 'It's a job. I'm lucky to get it, I suppose.'

Just before he climbed out of the car at the supermarket car park, he asked if he might call round sometime.

'Just to see if you've heard anything from Nicola?'

'Of course. Drop in any time, and we

can share any news we've had.'

What else could she say?

* * *

The pleasant sense of homecoming that Linda experienced when she entered the office surprised her. She'd worked there less than three months, but today she found it a relief to let family matters slip to the back of her mind and business concerns take over.

She'd asked her boss's permission to come in late to allow her to drive Nicola to the airport and see her off. Still, she felt embarrassed at arriving halfway through the morning.

Although she had seen Richard Mason a little testy from time to time, on the whole he was a good boss, considerate and polite.

Her sense of guilt increased when she saw him standing beside her desk taking a telephone call and scribbling down notes as he spoke. Doing her work.

9

He raised a hand in salute, however, as she hurried to hang up her jacket and she smiled back at him tentatively. He looked pleased about something. A good order, she hoped.

She hadn't been there long enough to learn much about him, or to discover why he should often be so tense. Did he, too, have family worries? She knew he had a teenage daughter, Karen, but he spoke of her with such affection that Linda didn't imagine that she could be the problem.

Now, however, there was a throb of barely concealed excitement in his voice and his honest eyes, for once, were smiling as he finished the call.

When he'd put down the phone and finished making notes, his gaze returned to her.

'OK?' he asked, unexpectedly concerned.

'Fine, thank you. She's off in good spirits.'

'But you? What about you? You don't look in such good spirits. Come on, a coffee will straighten us both out.'

'I'll get it!' she exclaimed as he headed towards the tiny kitchen, but in trying to reach it before him she only succeeded in getting in his way.

'Sorry!' they both said at once, laughing, then he politely ushered her through the doorway ahead of him.

As he leaned on the door-jamb watching her fill the kettle he told her about his hopes for a substantial order as a result of that telephone conversation. He seemed more relaxed and happier today than she'd ever seen him, she thought.

'That's wonderful!' she enthused, then muttered as she succeeded in spilling more water over the kettle than she was putting into it.

'Hey, your nerves are shot to pieces,' he observed kindly, taking the kettle from her. 'Even I could have made a better job of that!'

'Oh, I know!' she retorted over-brightly, and to her horror felt her eyes brimming with tears.

'Hey, now, what's the matter?' he asked in concern, and there was so much kindness in his voice that she couldn't stop the tears spilling over and trickling down her cheeks.

'I've got no idea!' She sounded puzzled. 'I had this weird sense of — oh, apprehension as I said goodbye to Nicola this morning. I've been a quivering wreck ever since.' But she knew that just telling this kindly man about it was making her feel better.

'It was just a mother's nerves, I'm sure,' he told her in a deliberately laid-back, comfortable sort of way. 'It's perfectly natural. Did you tell Nicola how you felt?'

'No, of course not! I couldn't have tried to explain anything so vague. The young ones would have laughed at me. And anyway, as you said, it's probably just a mother's natural anxiety.'

He nodded sympathetically.

'Of course it was. Look, what you need is a break. You've worked very hard since you came to me three months ago, and we've both been too busy to get to know each other. Would you consider coming out for a meal with me on Saturday night?'

Linda hesitated, sensing that their relationship had started to change. She wasn't sure she was ready for it.

'You're not baby-sitting on Saturday, are you?' he asked.

Linda quite often looked after her elder daughter, Gail's, two young children.

'No, but . . . ' Her eyes were troubled. Since Alan's death she'd never been out alone with a man.

'Look on it as a sort of working dinner,' Richard urged her, 'an opportunity to discuss all those things we never have time to here.'

'Oh, well . . . ' She nodded. On that basis she could certainly go. 'Well, thank you. That would be very nice.'

'Great! I think it'll do us both good.'

★ ★ ★

'It's good of you to come and baby-sit at such short notice, Mum.' Gail gave her mother an appreciative hug. 'You know I'm grateful. We'll not be late.' She shrugged into her jacket. 'It's just a meal and a few drinks with Sheila and Jack. They only phoned last night or I would have asked you sooner.'

'I couldn't have come if it had been tomorrow,' Linda told her a trifle sharply, glad she could say this with truth.

Linda suspected that Gail and Steve couldn't really afford to go out as often as they did. Steve had been made redundant two years ago and although he had found a new job it wasn't at all secure, and Linda worried about them wasting money when their circumstances were so unsettled.

Just then, Steve himself came in, carrying a pyjama-clad Emma.

'This young lady won't go to sleep,' he announced, placing her in Linda's welcoming arms. 'She wants to say goodnight to her granny all over again.'

'Will Granny read you another story, darling? Then maybe you'll fall asleep?'

'Yes, please!' Emma coughed then squirrelled down into Linda's lap, her thumb creeping towards her mouth.

The children, secure in their granny's love, barely noticed their parents' departure as five-year-old Christopher, who had been busy over by the window with a dumper truck, fetched Emma's favourite storybook, and even deigned to listen to a 'baby' story, provided he got one of his own choice later.

Linda, shifting Emma's weight in order to hold the book, thought she seemed too hot and wondered if that was why she was being more fractious than usual. Maybe she wasn't feeling well.

That would certainly explain why she hadn't been her usual self tonight. Emma, although only three, had already decided on her career. She was going to be a ballet dancer and she always treated her granny to a demonstration whenever she came to visit, turning herself into a ballerina and flitting about. Linda loved to watch the bright little soul. But tonight there had been no performance. She had been too tired.

'Are you feeling quite well, darling?' Linda asked her after she'd finished reading the story, but there was no reply. Emma was fast asleep.

Listening anxiously to the faintly wheezing respiration, Linda carried her up to bed.

Emma had always been a slightly asthmatic child, but Linda had some pet theories about food allergies and when she went downstairs she questioned Christopher about what they had had to eat that day.

She loved being with the children and felt quite lonely when Christopher had had his story and his bath and had gone obediently to bed. They were good children and she was proud of the way Gail was bringing them up, in spite of her having been such a young bride and mother.

Much later, Gail and Steve came in, looking happy, and both grateful to Linda for making their night out possible.

'I don't mind in the least,' Linda told them sincerely. 'I love the children. But . . . I was just thinking . . . ' She hesitated, desperately trying to be tactful, but feeling she had to speak her mind. 'If you're worrying about being made redundant again, don't you think you should be saving for a rainy day?'

Steve nodded glumly, but Gail was clearly annoyed.

'Are you saying we shouldn't have any fun? Don't you understand that the only way to cope with all the uncertainty is to go out occasionally and forget all about it?'

'Steady on, Gail — ' Steve intervened but before he could say any more, a wail came from above.

'Great — now Emma's awake!' Gail complained. 'Steve, would you please go up and see what's wrong.'

Steve leapt for the stairs and Gail swung round to her mother again.

'Well, I won't trouble you to babysit for us again,' she said huffily. 'I'll ask someone else! And maybe I shouldn't bring the children round to see you so often. You'll be telling me next I'm wasting petrol!'

'Don't be silly, Gail!' Linda tried to appear unruffled by her anger. 'You know very well what I meant. I was only thinking of you.'

But there was no placating her and Linda felt miserable as she drove home. The last thing she wanted was to fall out with her daughter, especially now Nicola was away. But Gail seemed to have forgotten how worried she'd been the last time Steve had been out of work.

Linda felt a pang of the old loneliness she had suffered so acutely after Alan's death and which she had thought was easing. It wasn't just his physical presence she missed. He had always been so willing to listen to her problems and help her sort out family disputes. Now there was no-one to confide in, no one to share the burden.

A Sense Of Belonging

Nicola stood on the shaded terrace of the Villa Ranieri, looking down on the enchanting coastline and the terraced slopes which were dotted with other villas nestling among the lemon groves, vines and olive trees.

She let her gaze follow an impossibly long serpentine of steps till they reached the shore and then allowed her eyes to feast on the intense emerald of the sea which shaded off to inky blue further out.

The water was busy with pleasure craft of every size and the hydrofoil was skimming past, full of holiday-makers bent on visiting other places along the coast.

She let out a sigh of pure pleasure. She'd been haunted by Italy all her life and now that she was here, she had an overwhelming sense of belonging.

Signor Ranieri, Carlo's grandfather, was the most charismatic man she had ever met though he wasn't tall and handsome in a conventional storybook hero way. Rather he was quite short and thick-set, with a broad face, wiry black hair generously sprinkled with silver and twinkling eyes the colour of deep, dark chocolate.

He was as kind as he was charming. Although he spoke English very well, he had decided that he must also help Nicola improve her Italian and already they had had several interesting chats during which he had gently schooled her.

She brought her attention back to the little boy beside her at the table, his nose buried in a glass of orange juice. Carlo especially loved the weekends because then his grandpa didn't go off to business in Naples.

When he put his empty glass down Nicola wiped the ring of orange from his mouth. She hoped she was looking after him with just the right degree of caring and discipline. Fortunately she'd had lots of practise in minding her sister's children.

Carlo was a special case, though, and it would be very easy to spoil him. He'd been only two years old when his mother and grandmother had been tragically killed in a plane crash — mercifully too young to really take in what had happened.

'*Nonno!*' Carlo yelled gleefully as his grandfather stepped on to the terrace. The child was out of his seat before Nicola could restrain him and hurtling towards the outstretched arms.

'*Buongiorno, Carlo!*'

'*Buongiorno, Nonno!*'

'*Buongiorno, Nicola!*' Giorgio called round Carlo's head as the child burrowed into his shoulder.

Nicola returned the greeting carefully.

As the manservant, Raimondo, came out with more fresh orange juice, coffee and rolls, Giorgio carried Carlo back to the table and reseated him on the cushion on his chair.

Raimondo cleared away the empty dishes and was about to take them back to the kitchen when Carlo wriggled down from his seat again, intent on accompanying him to visit Maria who did the cooking. It was something Carlo loved to do and nobody stopped him.

'Carlo's father has just telephoned from Rome, Nicola, to see how you are settling in. Are you quite happy with us?'

'Oh, yes, signore! It's beautiful here and Carlo is adorable. It would be very easy to spoil him.'

'I know. It is a temptation. One feels that way especially in the circumstances. But my son wants him to grow up strong and independent, so we must not make him soft.'

'Has Carlo had an Italian nanny until now?' Nicola asked.

'Yes, of course. Francesca has been with the family for many years. In fact, she was nurse to Carlo's father, and his brothers and sisters. But when she had to go into hospital for an operation, it was necessary to find someone else to care for Carlo while I am working. My son wants Carlo to start learning English while he is still very young, so it makes sense to employ an English nanny.'

He beamed fondly at Nicola. 'I feel we are very lucky to have found you.'

Nicola smiled back warmly. 'I think I am the lucky one, signore,' she assured him.

Soon Carlo returned with sticky mouth and fingers and Nicola rose to take him off to wash.

'Are we going to the beach today, Grandpa?' Carlo asked.

'Well, this is Saturday, certainly, Carlo, and we usually go to the beach on Saturdays. But I have someone coming to see me this morning, so who is going to take you today? Nicola is supposed to have a rest on Saturdays. Wouldn't you rather play in your own swimming pool today?'

'I can take him,' Nicola offered quickly.

'No, Nicola! It is always to be your day off. It was specially arranged because I am here. Now, let me see . . . I could, perhaps, take you later.'

'Oh, please let me take him if it will help,' Nicola pleaded. 'I haven't been here long enough to earn a day off!'

'Nicola can take me,' Carlo declared loftily, 'and I can show her the way! I'm four!'

They laughed in delight at him.

'It is true, you are four,' his grandfather agreed solemnly. 'Then I suppose that settles it.'

Nicola soon realised that she must have been mad to say, so confidently, that she could drive the unfamiliar Italian car along the coast road to the village where Giorgio's close friend, Luigi, owned the hotel with the beach.

Not that there was any danger of getting lost so long as the sea was on her right and she was heading south. But she was driving, for the first time, on the 'wrong' side of the road — a hazardous road, what's more, peppered with blind corners and fast drivers.

She was wringing with nervous perspiration and wondered how soon she could jump into the sea to cool down.

Carlo was fastened into his seat in the back of the car but bounced in it excitedly as he kept up a flow of instructions that she didn't really need since there was nowhere else to go but onwards.

As far as the winding road would allow, she encouraged all the other drivers to pass her. There was one car, however, which, though very powerful looking, failed to take advantage of her invitations to pass. She shrugged. Perhaps he was in no hurry.

In fact, as she slowed down to turn into the car park of the hotel, the black car with its tinted glass slowed down, too.

So preoccupied had she been with driving a strange car in these difficult conditions, it was only then that it dawned on her that the saloon had been a constant feature in her rear-view mirror.

With a sickening sensation in the pit of her stomach, she sensed that the car had been following them.

★ ★ ★

Richard had taken Linda to one of his favourite restaurants, an informal little French-style bistro by the river, for supper, and now he smiled encouragingly across the table at her.

'I can see you've got something on your mind. Why don't you tell me about it? You shouldn't keep things bottled up, you know.'

'Oh, it's just family stuff. I don't want to bore you with my affairs,' she said earnestly.

'You could never do that.' His voice was quietly persuasive. 'One day I'd like to see the sadness leave your face.'

'I'm not at all sad,' she insisted. 'I'm

enjoying the novelty of eating out . . . Oh!' She put a hand to her mouth in sudden understanding. 'I see what Gail meant. You do feel different when you come out among other people who are having a good time.'

She looked so perturbed that he asked, 'Gail — that's your daughter, right? And have you fallen out with her? Is that it?'

She had to admit that it was true.

'But I don't want to talk about it right now. I'm enjoying the super food and this lovely place so much.'

'Well, that's good.' He leaned towards her encouragingly. 'Tell me about Nicola first, then. That shouldn't be so difficult.'

'Oh, she seems to be fine. She phoned me on her first night out there, quite enchanted with everything. Apparently Signor Ranieri — he's the grandfather of the child she's nanny to — is very charming and kind. For instance he's insisted that she must phone home as often as she likes, so I don't feel at all cut off from her as I thought I might.

'The little boy, Carlo, is mischievous but very lovable. He seems to be quite a character for his age. Nicola says it would be very easy to spoil the little chap. He has no mother, you see — apparently she died along with Carlo's grandmother in a tragic accident.' Linda shook her head sadly. 'It's a terrible thing for a child to be deprived of his mother.'

'Yes, I have a lot of sympathy with anyone in that position,' he returned quietly.

She suddenly realised how tactless she had been.

'Oh, Richard, I'm so sorry!' She stretched out her hand to touch his. 'What have I said? Did Karen's mother — ?'

'No, she didn't die . . . ' He paused, then hastened back to the previous subject. 'Well, Nicola certainly seems to have landed on her feet!'

'Oh yes! I've had Fraser round a

couple of times, desperate for news of her. I think he's rather jealous that she's having all the fun while he's stuck here in a boring dead-end job!'

Richard laughed. 'At least he's in work, earning some money. I hope I'll never be unemployed again as long as I live. It eats away at you.'

'It must be a dreadful experience.'

'It's a body blow,' he agreed. 'But I suppose I might have coped better if I hadn't still been reeling from my wife walking out on me for another man.'

'Oh, good heavens! What a terrible thing!' Linda exclaimed, not really knowing what to say.

He laughed a little dryly.

'Life's all about confidence, I believe. When you've taken a knock you become vulnerable so that one set-back then leads to another . . . It's often the way.'

'I'm afraid that's what might be happening with my son-in-law,' Linda commented, and found herself telling

30

him all about the pain and bewilderment she'd brought down on her own head by her interference in Gail and Steve's lives.

'I meant to be so tactful, too,' she mourned, then shrugged. 'But I don't know why I'm telling you all this! I didn't mean to burden you with my troubles.'

He patted her hand in a gesture of support.

'I'm glad you did. It makes me feel you trust me. But now let's see if we can get these worries into perspective . . . '

'There is no other perspective!' Linda broke in. 'I'm not going to see my darling grandchildren so often and it's entirely my own big-mouthed fault!'

'Try not to worry,' he soothed. 'These family tiffs always blow over. Gail was probably feeling guilty. Maybe the evening cost more than she'd calculated and you hit a raw spot. We always lash out at the ones we love most.'

However, Linda wasn't so sure. He hadn't seen the look in Gail's eyes.

Still, his kind concern enabled her to summon up a smile and resolve to be an interested and entertaining companion for the rest of the evening.

'Anyway, enough about me — what about you? It was brave of you to start up on your own when you'd been made redundant. How did it come about?'

'Well, I had an idea, you see — more than an idea.' Enthusiasm brought a vital sparkle to his eyes. 'I had devised this electronic gadget and I decided that instead of selling my idea, I would try to market it on my own using my redundancy money. And the rest, as they say, is history.'

'And you set it all up with a divorce to go through?'

'Yes. And my daughter to support.'

'Ah, yes, your daughter — how old is Karen now?'

'She's seventeen. It came as a shock to both of us when her mother left. She gave me no warning before she moved in with another man and told me our marriage was over. I refused to believe her at first, and even when she kept repeating it each time as she came to remove more of her clothes. Karen and I just kept on expecting her to come home.'

'And Karen came down on your side of the fence?'

'Oh, definitely. We're very close. She's a lovely girl . . . but that's not to say she doesn't worry me sometimes.'

'Teenagers are always a worry,' Linda agreed with feeling. 'But it gets better — most of the time, anyway!' she added with a rueful smile.

'I hope you're right!'

'So you got it all together in spite of everything?' she asked, returning to the topic of the business.

'Obviously I took advice about feasibility, but . . . yes. It was scary at first, mind. You see, Janette had finally demanded that I see a solicitor with a view to a divorce and I was struggling with this denial thing. I wouldn't accept that it was happening. I was still trying to convince myself that I was a single parent when the redundancy struck.'

'It's something like being bereaved,' Linda said. 'Perhaps it was good that you had the demands of building up your own new company to throw yourself into.'

'There's no doubt about it.' He laughed. 'But I'll never forget all those sleepless nights!'

They talked business exclusively after that, a subject that totally absorbed them until it was time to pay the bill and head home.

As they drove, Linda glanced at her watch, a gesture that Richard noticed.

'Not worried about the time, are you?' he asked.

'No, it's not that. I'm just wondering if it's too late to call my mother. I always give her a ring at the weekend. But I expect she'll have gone to bed. I can't help worrying about her. She's always getting into some scrape or other.'

'Linda!' he scolded. 'Not more worrying!'

She laughed and gave a rueful grimace.

'Well, she is my mother! I'll drive over and see her tomorrow,' she decided.

They were pulling up at her bungalow and she wondered if she should invite him in.

'Would you like to come in for a coffee or a drink?' she asked tentatively.

'I'd love to!' he agreed briskly.

As he followed her into the kitchen, he chuckled.

'You'd better let me fill the kettle!' he joked, harking back to the incident in the office that afternoon, and she found herself laughing quite naturally. The employer-employee restraint between them was slowly melting. They were more comfortable with each other, more like old friends.

They had just settled down before the fire with their coffee when they were startled by the ringing of the phone.

'At this hour!' Linda jumped up, spilling coffee into her saucer. 'I hope nothing's happened to my mother!'

But it wasn't her mother, it was Gail . . .

'Mum! Could you come round and stay with Christopher? Steve's on night duty and I've had to call an ambulance for Emma — she's having a really bad asthma attack. The little love can't breathe. I've got to go with her . . .'

★ ★ ★

Nicola was beginning to appreciate that the siesta in Mediterranean countries wasn't just an indulgence. By the time lunch was over the heat was overwhelming and she was glad to retreat, like everyone else, behind closed shutters.

She lay on the bed, enjoying the dim coolness, and reviewed the morning. It had been fun playing on the beach with Carlo and the little friends he had quickly made among the other children staying at the hotel owned by Giorgio's friend, Luigi. They had parked there and gone in to speak to Luigi before going down on to his strip of beach.

When Luigi had come out on to the steps to the beach with them, the car which Nicola had imagined was following them had disappeared.

She had breathed a sigh of relief. Obviously her imagination had been working overtime!

She closed her eyes and stretched out luxuriously on the huge bed. Her bedroom at home would have fitted into one corner of the room she had been given, and her spacious bathroom with its cream-coloured marble and gold fittings delighted her.

Giorgio had said she was free until tomorrow, so later, when it was cooler, she would open the shutters and sit at the ornate desk and write to Fraser and perhaps to her mother and Gail, too. Phone calls were all right but you often forgot what you meant to say . . . And on that thought she drifted off to sleep.

That night, after a pleasant dinner with Giorgio, Nicola decided to go for a stroll and post the three letters she had written in the early evening. She had enjoyed describing her impressions and experiences so far and was anxious to send them on their way.

When she came back the garden looked so inviting that she couldn't bear the thought of going inside.

The steep nature of the coast dictated that the villa's gardens were laid out in terraces. Shrubs and flowers, some rare and exotic, planted with artistry, bloomed everywhere. The swimming pool, with its underwater lighting, looked like an emerald lagoon.

Beyond, the hillside plunged away so steeply that the garden seemed to hang there in space, before the star-spangled sky.

This was made for lovers, Nicola thought romantically, and her heart ached with longing for Fraser.

The days were OK. She was enchanted with Carlo and loved looking after him. But in the evenings, when she was alone, she missed Fraser so much, missed his arms around her, his warm, gentle kisses.

Although it was quite late, she was reluctant to go in just yet. Instead she wandered along the twisting paths towards the stone bench which had been placed in the shadow of an ancient olive tree, where she could be alone with her thoughts for just a little longer.

She didn't see the man already sitting there until it was almost too late. She jumped back, startled.

'Who are you?' she blurted out in English, just as the stranger asked the same question of her.

Before she could move, he had taken her hands in his and drawn her towards him.

'*Stai zitto!*' he whispered. 'Keep quiet.' And he held one of his fingers against her lips.

Her knees threatened to give way with fear and she found herself sagging against him. Who was he? Was there some connection with the car that had followed her that afternoon?

Signor Ranieri, Signor Ranieri! She wailed inwardly. Please help me!

A stream of rapid Italian was being poured into her ears, the deep, warm voice setting the hairs on the back of her neck tingling.

'Don't scream! Don't be afraid! Stay calm!'

Stay calm! Huh!

Then her prayer was miraculously answered. They heard footsteps on the path above them, recognisably those of the signore.

Thank heaven! Her heart soared with relief.

'Keep quiet! Don't say a word!' Her captor's voice was urgent. 'Meet me here at midnight or you will endanger Carlo's life. Do you understand?'

As she tried to nod, she was abruptly released.

'Yes!' she croaked, but it was to empty air. The man had vanished.

Ironically, the signore's footsteps

then faded as though he was returning to the house. Angels watching over me, Nicola thought hysterically.

As reaction set in like an icy shower, and the garden seemed to sway about her, her knees seemed to give way beneath her and she sank on to the stone bench. She was horribly aware, with a fresh knotting of her stomach, that she had a decision to make. Should she obey the stranger's instructions and return here at midnight?

No! Her mind screamed. She couldn't possibly do that!

She peered at her watch in the darkness. Almost eleven o'clock? It could be. Dinner was eaten so late here.

She tried to remember what the man's parting shot had been. If she didn't come — Carlo would be in danger . . .

No! She covered her mouth with both hands. She couldn't allow anything to happen to Carlo!

★ ★ ★

At one minute to twelve Nicola was back sitting on the bench. He came stealthily out of the shadows once more and seated himself beside her, sending a thrill of unease through her.

'*Buona sera!*' he murmured in a normal-sounding voice.

'Good evening,' Nicola replied nervously. 'What is it you want? I'll do anything you ask, if only you'll leave the child alone.'

'You mean that?' His breath caught oddly. 'You mean . . . you would sacrifice yourself for Carlo?'

'If there was no other option,' she agreed firmly.

'*Mio dio!*' he said in wonder. 'I can't believe this is true. A reliable nanny! A totally devoted English nanny!'

Gently he grasped her shoulders and turned her so that she had to look at him.

He had one of those ridiculously good-looking Latin faces with smooth, deeply-tanned skin, close-cropped black hair, a white smile that wouldn't have

42

disgraced a film star and eyes the colour of wickedly dark coffee.

'I am Carlo's father,' he said.

Astonishment froze Nicola for a moment.

'Then why did you scare the life out of me like that?' she demanded, every inch of her quivering with outrage.

He rubbed his temples. 'I'm sorry, *signorina*, but I didn't want to startle the household. My father mustn't know I am here. I've gone to ground, you see.'

'No, I don't see! What do you mean, 'gone to ground'? You make it sound like you're some sort of gangster! Don't you want to talk to your father? To your son?'

'Of course I do — but I daren't. I'm working undercover. I'm an undercover agent for the carabinieri.'

To Nicola it sounded ridiculously like shades of 007! But then again, maybe it wasn't so ridiculous. The carabinieri, she knew, were different from the British police. She thought they were

43

more like the FBI and somehow attached to the army.

'I'm tracking down some very dangerous men. I'm reckoned to be very good at catching criminals and I will not rest until these ones are apprehended.'

His tone was chilling and Nicola shivered as he went on, 'I came to warn you to look after Carlo very carefully. These people are ruthless. No one is safe from them.'

His eyes passed over her slowly.

'I don't know why, but I feel I can trust you. Don't tell my father — or anyone — you have seen me. I shouldn't be here.' He stood up. 'Just, please . . . ' His voice grew husky. 'I had to see you for myself. I had to tell you . . . Please keep my *bambino* safe!'

And then Angelo Ranieri disappeared as silently as he had come, before she had time to speak. Before she had time to tell him about the car. Before . . .

Angelo Ranieri! Some angel!

Family Troubles . . .

Saturday morning found Linda back in her own home but with a weekend guest in the person of her five-year-old grandson, Christopher.

Just a simple summer cold had triggered off his little sister's asthma attack. Linda had arrived at their home in time to see Gail, white-faced, climbing into the ambulance after the paramedics had carried Emma in, one holding an oxygen mask in place.

Gail had known, of course, that she must at all costs appear calm and not let Emma sense her panic, and Linda's heart had gone out to Gail as she recognised the noble effort she was making to hide her concern from the child.

Christopher had been asleep in bed, blissfully unaware of the drama, but Linda had sat up all night, too anxious

45

to sleep. She had tried to read and had made numerous cups of coffee, while remaining constantly alert for the ringing of the telephone.

In the morning Steven had come home at last, returning from his night-shift via the hospital.

While Linda had got him some breakfast he had brought her up to date with Emma's condition.

The medical staff had taken good care of the child, helping her to breath with the aid of a nebuliser.

'The doctor was very kind,' Steve had told her. 'They've managed without putting Em on a ventilator. But I'd like to get one of those nebulisers to have in the house, so that if she ever gets so distressed again, we've got it here. It's awful to see your child suffering like that and not be able to do anything for them.'

He had taken a deep, gulping breath to steady himself.

'Gail's going to stay with her until she stabilises and until they stabilise the medication.' He had looked at her appealingly.

'Linda, do you think you could possibly have Christopher to stay with you for a couple of days? I have to go back to the hospital — Gail needs some things. But I don't think I'm safe to drive till I've crashed out for a couple of hours.

'But, could you — would you be at home if we needed you? Emma's not out of the woods yet.'

'Of course I'll have Christopher,' Linda had agreed readily. 'And you must come and eat with us this evening if you're still on your own.'

So now she was getting breakfast for her young house-guest and doing her best to act like nothing was wrong.

'Porridge or cornflakes, Christopher?' she said, rooting around in her kitchen cupboards. 'There are some rice things here but they might be soft. Must have been here since your last visit.' She chuckled. She didn't want Christopher sensing any anxiety.

'Any free gifts in the packets, Gran?'

'Let's have a look — no, it's coupons you have to collect. D'you want them?'

They heard the noise of an engine and then the crunch of wheels on the gravel drive, and a moment later Fraser was at the back door. Christopher's eyes widened at the sight of him in his black motorbike leathers.

'Hello, Mrs Gray! Hi, Christopher!'

'Come in, Fraser. I'm just going to have some coffee — like some?'

'Thanks, Mrs Gray. Any more word from Nicola?'

'Nothing new. She said she was going to write some letters, so you can expect to hear from her very soon, I'm sure.'

Fraser seated himself in the breakfast corner beside Christopher.

'Cheers, Chris!' He toasted the youngster before tasting his coffee. 'Where's your sister today, then?'

He was stunned when they told him all that had happened.

'That's really tough,' he sympathised. 'I had meant to visit my mother today,' Linda went on with a sigh. 'But Steve's coming for a meal later and he wants us to stay around in case Gail phones . . . ' Her voice trailed away for a moment before she added, 'I'm a bit worried about my mother, though. I haven't been able to reach her on the phone.'

'Leave it to me,' Fraser said unexpectedly. 'I'll nip over on the bike and see how she is.'

'Fraser! It's thirty miles. I can't let you do that!'

'Why not? I'd like to meet Nicola's gran. I'll just pop over, check that she's all right, then come back and put your mind at rest.'

'But it's your day off, Fraser!'

'Days off are dead dull when Nicola's not here,' he said simply.

★   ★   ★

'Mrs Moretti?' Fraser asked uncertainly. He had found the address, and now sensed somehow that the attractive

49

lady pacing impatiently up and down outside was Nicola's grandmother.

Wearing slacks of a cheerful plaid and a navy sweatshirt bearing the print of a stately home, she hastened to where he still sat astride his motorbike at the kerb.

'Thank goodness you're here at last!' she exclaimed.

'How did you know I was coming?' he asked, bemused. Linda had said she couldn't get through on the phone.

'They said they were sending a young man,' she told him as she climbed on to the back of the bike, slinging her bulging shoulder bag round to her back.

Bemused, he handed her Nicola's helmet which lived on the bike.

'I thought,' she said as she fastened the helmet confidently, 'it would be a car, but this is much more fun.'

'Where to, then?' Fraser revved up, expecting to be told they were going to Linda's, but —

'To the centre of the village, of

course. You can park near the village green.'

'Your daughter was worried because she couldn't reach you on the phone!' he shouted as they roared down the street.

'What's that about the phone? I can't hear you! They can't expect to get me when I spend all my time at The Rose.'

The Rose? Fraser supposed that was Mrs Moretti's local.

'The Rose? That's where we're going?' he queried.

'Well, of course! But we'll leave the bike and walk there, won't we?'

'Sure,' Fraser agreed cheerfully. He knew those restful, atmospheric old inns, redolent of old wood, ale and roast beef. Suddenly feeling hungry, he began to fantasise about the pint and the ploughman's lunch he might have when they got there.

But — 'It looks all boarded up!' he exclaimed indignantly when the bike was parked and they were strolling down the village street.

'It is!' Gwen's indignation matched his. 'Look — even the stonearched coach-entrance is barricaded. It's vandalism, that's what it is! We'll have to go round the next corner, along the lane and over the wall.'

Fraser looked down at her, his face a study in bewilderment. He was wondering if all would become clear shortly — or if Nicola's gran was simply seriously eccentric.

A long, high wall ran the length of the lane, punctuated by an assortment of gates and doors. When they came to the stretch that backed The Rose, the door into the lane appeared bolted and barred.

He rapped loudly on the door and, after a moment, they heard a key grating in the lock. Then the door creaked open six inches, revealing a pleasant elderly face sporting a small moustache, and about on a level with Fraser's own.

'Gwen! At last! Where have you been?'

'Let us in, Rodney, quickly. The young man Agnes was sending has only just arrived. This is the colonel, dear — Colonel Bingham, the mainstay of our campaign.'

As they walked towards the building, Fraser thought he ought to have another try at explaining his arrival that morning.

'Mrs Moretti, I wasn't sent by anyone called Agnes,' he said quickly. 'I came on behalf of your daughter, Linda. She was worried about you because she couldn't get you on the phone.'

Gwen stopped walking and looked up at him. 'Who are you, then?'

'I'm Nicola's boyfriend.'

'Nicola's boyfriend? I see. I wonder what's happened to Ag's nephew then?'

Fraser was looking in amazement at the building as they approached. It seemed disused and in very poor repair.

'It's not an inn at all?' he queried.

'It hasn't been one since before the war. It's utterly derelict now,' Gwen explained. 'At one time it was a coaching inn called the Rose and Crown — a lovely place, it was, back then. But over the years it's fallen into disrepair. The council used to use the upstairs for meetings and stored trestle tables and benches and things like that downstairs — but then they got their new premises, and it's been allowed to go to rack and ruin.'

It was dark inside the building which, by some secret system of the colonel's, they entered through a cellar door.

The light from a torch cast a dull glow on old whitewashed stone walls and empty bottle racks.

In the centre of the unevenly-flagged floor stood an ancient-looking wooden table onto which Gwen thankfully dumped her bag.

'I've brought some food for us,' she announced cheerfully.

She poured soup from a flask into mugs which were kept there, then produced rolls filled with cheese and pickle which did much to restore

Fraser's morale.

It was over this packed lunch that he was brought fully into the picture.

Seated on a stool and leaning on the table, he listened as Gwen explained how she had been infuriated when she had read in the local paper that the old inn, whose façade contributed so much to the character of the village street, was to be pulled down and replaced by a modern block of flats.

'There's no reason why The Rose can't be made into modern flats,' said the colonel, 'only retaining the character of the front of the building.'

The developers had resisted this suggestion, however, and Gwen, having had no co-operation from them or from the local council, had started writing to every organisation concerned with preserving England's historic heritage.

Most local folk shared her views, she had learned, but sadly most were too busy to concern themselves with launching a campaign to save the façade of the building. However, in time a group had emerged, mostly retired persons.

Having learned recently that the builders were ready to move in and present the world with a fait accompli, Gwen's group had decided that the only way to delay things was to squat in the building until, it was hoped, a preservation notice could be slapped on it.

'Not only is it a beautiful example of a seventeenth-century inn,' she told Fraser now, 'it's haunted!'

'Wow! Who by?' he asked.

'She's a serving wench,' the colonel informed him. 'A servant who hid some Royalists from Cromwell's army after the battle of Marston Moor, and who was put in prison where she later died.'

'It's said she comes back and haunts this cellar where she hid the king's men.'

Gwen looked around the gloomy area. 'There must have been a large cupboard or something like that in here in those days.'

'Perhaps over there.' Fascinated by the tale, Fraser pointed to the most likely dark corner, and almost leapt out of his skin when a piece of wood decided at that moment to detach itself from the wall and clatter loudly to the floor.

'Er — I don't think you should stay here alone, Mrs Moretti,' Fraser said earnestly. 'It's spooky. Besides, nothing will happen now till Monday.'

'That's true,' Colonel Bingham agreed. 'The building trades, demolishers and so on, knock off at the weekend.'

'Besides, Mrs Moretti,' Fraser pressed his advantage, 'I think Linda would like to see you. Emma's in hospital . . .'

'In hospital?' Gwen suddenly looked anxious. 'Oh, good heavens! What's wrong? Is it her asthma?' She turned to the colonel. 'Rodney, I must go. Will you stay here?'

'Yes, all right. But will you come back tomorrow? And I'm hoping that by

Monday morning you'll have heard from English Heritage or the National Trust.'

'Yes, let's hope so.' Gwen got up hurriedly and started tidying up. 'Fraser, could you possibly take me to Linda's on your motorbike, d'you think?'

'Of course — I'd be delighted.'

★   ★   ★

Apart from the background worry about Emma, Linda couldn't remember a day that had passed so pleasantly. Keeping Christopher entertained completely absorbed her.

In the afternoon, having heard nothing from the hospital and taking it that no news was good news, they made a hasty dash to the supermarket to shop for supper.

Steve would probably be hungry when he arrived, Linda reasoned, but she must consider Christopher's preferences too.

Christopher liked pasta. They discussed the matter and settled on lasagne, lots of salad, chips and extra vegetables.

Linda, with Christopher's help, had almost finished organising the meal when the characteristic sounds of Fraser's bike arriving reached them.

'Fraser!' Christopher rushed out excitedly with Linda following to call out in her turn, 'Mum!' in delighted amazement. 'Oh, look, Christopher! Look who Fraser has brought!'

As soon as Gwen had clambered off the bike, Linda threw her arms round her, suddenly realising how much her presence at that moment meant to her.

'Thank you, Fraser!' she called to the lad. 'You will stay for supper with us, won't you? It's the least I can do.'

Gwen bent down and gave Christopher, who had climbed on to the bike to see what it was like to be a biker, a bear hug. Then she turned back to Linda.

'Now, tell me all about Emma. Any word?'

Briefly Linda told her all she knew, but soon Steve arrived with the good news that Emma was breathing more comfortably now and when he'd left the hospital, Gail and Emma had both been sound asleep.

Linda and Gwen nodded approvingly at each other. Sleep — always the best healer.

Over supper, Linda looked round her dining table with a real sense of well-being. It was like old times having five people sitting together enjoying a meal she had prepared for them.

They sat talking long into the evening, until Christopher grew very sleepy and it was time for his bedtime story.

Gwen had decided to stay the night, so Linda's sense of contentment and security continued even after Steve had left for home and Fraser had ridden off into the night.

* ★ ★

'And that's the Torre dello Ziro,' Signor Ranieri told Nicola, pointing to the most splendid of the guardian towers along the coast.

He had insisted on taking her to a concert at Ravello because he considered that she was looking pale and anxious and quite overdoing this business of not letting Carlo out of her sight. So tonight, they had left Carlo safely in bed with Anna, the maid, nearby in case he should waken.

They had left early in order to see something of the area and to have dinner before the concert, and the signore had also invited some young company for Nicola, Franco and Madelena, Angelo's closest friends.

From their vantage point the mountain descended towards the sea in cliffs with a broad terrace between them that levelled out where the tower stood.

'I have been told it is the tower in which the Duchess of Malfi was murdered,' Franco announced, and Nicola shivered. She thought it looked sinister in the evening light.

The round walls sloped inwards to a protruding ring of stone, above which it rose vertically. She'd seen many of those towers along the coast, some square, some round like this one.

'But you don't have to worry about being taken into it, Madelena,' teased Franco. 'You're too fat! It involves wriggling through a narrow tunnel in the wall. Two and a half metres. Very claustrophobic. The signorina could do it, she is slim enough.'

Madelena looked down at her shapely curves with a contented smile, and Nicola thought it must be wonderful to have so close a relationship with somebody that you knew when what sounded like an insult to others was really a secret compliment.

'I suppose you and Angelo have done it?' Madalena asked.

'Of course! When we were boys. We were dare-devils!'

'Always up to mischief,' Giorgio remarked complacently as he turned the car on to the winding road up to Ravello, perched a thousand feet almost sheer above sea level.

'The concert is to be staged on the belvedere of the Villa Rufolo, the most famous monument in Ravello,' he added a moment later.

Giorgio had chosen the restaurant of a fashionable hotel for supper, and the meal was delicious, like all the Italian cooking which Nicola had enjoyed since coming out to the Mediterranean. The whole place was buzzing with life with many people meeting before the concert, and the atmosphere was one of excited anticipation.

'How are you getting on with Carlo?' Madelena asked Nicola later in the powder room as they tidied their hair and reapplied their lipstick at the mirror.

'Oh, I love him! He's a super little boy,' Nicola replied.

'It was terrible about his mother. Rosa was my closest friend.'

63

That was all Madalena said before they rejoined the men to go on to the concert.

After walking along the tree-lined avenue, they inspected the famous Moorish cloister, strolling round it, admiring the delicate twin pillars arched over with swirling intricate designs.

The foursome were carried on the scent of the flowers to the belvedere with its fantastic view of the coastline. But Nicola felt she was on an emotional seesaw. She didn't know whether to revel in the glory of the evening or to weep for a girl whose life had been tragically cut short.

★ ★ ★

The orchestra played on a large platform suspended out over the cliff on scaffolding. The musicians had their backs to the sea and faced the audience who sat in the garden among the flowerbeds and fountains.

It was the first outdoor concert Nicola had ever attended and it couldn't have been a more magical experience. There were selections from Wagner, Vivaldi and Verdi and a superb tenor sang some of Alfredo's arias from La Traviata.

Nicola felt herself transported out of the real world and only came back down to earth to join in the rapturous and prolonged applause at the end of the programme.

Then their little group was being propelled amidst the crush of concert-goers out of the gardens and once again along the avenue.

Back in the piazza, now thronged with people, Giorgio said they were to wait there for him and he would bring the car.

'It will take some time,' was Franco's opinion when the signore had left. 'Shall I try to get you girls a drink?'

He didn't wait for an answer but dashed away to elbow his way into the throng.

Suddenly there was a series of loud cracks like gunfire on the far side of the square and every eye turned in that direction. There was a surge as people rushed over to see what was happening, and even Madelena pressed forward to get a better view.

Left alone at the back of the crowd, Nicola almost fainted when a remembered voice whispered in her ear, 'Did you enjoy the concert?'

She whirled round. The voice was his but the figure beside her was quite unrecognisable as Angelo, heavily disguised as he was as a tired old peasant.

'What are you doing here?' she whispered.

'Working. Don't come here again. This is not a healthy place for anyone connected with me.'

'But . . . ' Before she could say any more, he had melted into the crowd and was gone.

Making Headlines

A wan and tired little Emma was driven home from hospital on Monday. Steve had gone to collect them and had to wait while Gail received instructions from the doctor.

'He was telling me how lucky we are that asthma awareness and therapy have advanced so tremendously in recent years,' Gail told Steve as she settled into her seat at last and they drove out of the hospital grounds.

'Well, we'll just have to take extra good care of you, darling, won't we?' Steve said over his shoulder to Emma, sitting rather listlessly in her child seat. 'Don't you worry, pet, you'll grow out of it, I'm sure. What age are you now?'

'Daddy! You know I'm three and a bit!' Emma's indignant exclamation made her cough and Gail gave him an annoyed look for being the trigger.

'I was just wondering if you're old enough to become a swimming star or a cricketer yet,' he apologised, before going on to tell them about various sporting celebrities who had not allowed asthma to be an obstacle in their lives.

Gail sighed. 'I've to be more vigorous than ever in my cleaning, the doctor says. I told him how much vacuuming I already do, including Emma's bed. Oh, and our standard cleaner's no good. We need a more sophisticated one with a micro filter . . . '

He grimaced. 'That sounds like it'll be expensive.'

Now wasn't the time to tell her about the cut-backs at the factory. Better say nothing till they were home and Emma was settled.

Emma was propped up on the sofa with a colouring book when Christopher came home from school.

'Hi, Em!' he greeted her carelessly before tearing into the kitchen where Gail was unloading the washing machine.

'Can I have some crisps, Mum?'

'Can I have some crisps, *please*,' she reminded him, then, 'Anyway, there aren't any. How about a biscuit? But first come and give me a hug and tell me how you got on while we were in hospital.' She held out her arms to him, but he dodged past her and took up a defiant stance, his back to the door.

'I don't want a biscuit, I want crisps!' he shouted. 'Can I have money to go and buy some, then?'

'No, you can't,' Gail said quietly. 'You've had your pocket money.'

She sighed inwardly. It wasn't like Christopher to be stroppy, but she supposed she ought to have expected some reaction to the amount of attention Emma had been getting recently.

'I missed you, Christopher,' she told him gently. 'How did you get on at Gran's?'

'I splashed water on the floor and I pulled up all her flowers and I tore the roof off her house and then I rode away on Fraser's motorbike — and I hid.'

'Really?'

'Yes! And she gave me crisps!'

'In spite of all that?'

'Before. And then we had a party. Fraser and Great-gran and Daddy came. Can I have a party?'

'We'll have to see. Wait till Emma's better.'

'No! Now!'

'Now? This minute?'

'Tomorrow. And I want a kitten to play with.'

Gail tried to explain why they couldn't risk having a cat in the house but, of course, it was the wrong moment to expect Christopher to be reasonable.

She prayed that Steve would come home soon and take the boy to the play park or kick a ball with him in the garden. Christopher was feeling neglected and needed to have someone's undivided attention for a spell. But right now she had to get Emma's bed linen out on the line.

'Come out into the garden with me while I hang out the washing,' she coaxed.

But Christopher had other ideas and said he would rather watch TV. Well, at least it would keep him amused, she thought.

However, when she came in again, while she couldn't hear the TV she *could* hear some rumpus going on in the living-room and Emma coughing and wheezing.

Her heart froze with horror when she went into the room. Christopher, having snatched away Emma's book, was running round the room waving it above his head with Emma vainly trying to catch him.

'Christopher! Stop that at once!' Gail found herself screaming. 'What on earth do you think you're doing? D'you want to kill Emma?'

'Yes!' he yelled in bitter defiance, throwing down the book and running out of the room.

What a dilemma! But although she

knew she ought to go after Christopher, first Gail had to help Emma before another attack came on too badly.

Her hands were trembling as she soothed the child and tried to remember all she must do to help her use her inhaler properly.

'Breathe out gently. Now close your lips round the mouthpiece . . . '

Tears of worry filled her eyes. What was happening to her family?

It was with a surge of relief that she heard Steve's key in the door. Thank goodness he was home early!

'Steve! Could you come in here?'

'Not now, Gail . . . '

He sounded strange. Puzzled, she sat Emma down carefully on the settee and went out to him.

'What is it? What's wrong?'

'Pending further cuts,' he told her with a deep sigh, 'we're working a three-day week.'

★ ★ ★

It's only that old Monday morning feeling but I'm having it on Tuesday instead, Linda scolded herself as she struggled to settle down to work after her hectic weekend and having Monday off.

In no time, however, as she commanded total concentration, a satisfactory pile of letters awaited Richard's signature.

It was nearing lunch-time when he finally put in an appearance and asked her how things had gone.

It took her a moment to recall what he was referring to but then she remembered that the last time they had spoken it had been on a personal level, when he had insisted on driving her to Gail's house, told her to take Monday off, and had made her promise to get in touch with him if there was anything else he could do to help.

She had been so distracted with worry about Emma and, in fact, with the whole family drama, that she could scarcely remember saying goodnight to him, far less thanking him, before he'd driven off. Well, she could put that right now.

'Oh, Mr Mason . . . Richard,' she substituted hastily in answer to his look. 'I didn't thank you properly that night. You were so understanding. I'm sorry our chat was cut short.'

'Where were we?' he inquired humorously.

'Where were we?'

'In our conversation.'

'Oh.' She put her hand up to her brow. 'I can't think.'

'Shall I remind you?' He grinned at her, his eyes twinkling.

'I wish you would!'

'You were telling me about your mother. Worrying that you weren't keeping proper tabs on her. You were convinced the call was from her, in some bother. Remember?'

'I do. You're absolutely right. And as for Mum getting herself into hot water . . . well, it's only a matter of time!'

As they chatted, Richard perched

himself on the edge of her desk in a characteristic relaxed pose, swinging one foot, and as they laughed together Linda experienced a lightening of her gloomy mood.

'And how about your little grand-daughter?'

She was relieved to report that Emma's progress was satisfactory.

Suddenly the door from the vestibule was flung open and Karen, his daughter, burst in.

'Well!' she exclaimed.

Astonishment held Richard silent for a moment, then he began to unfold himself from his perch.

'Hello, Karen — what's up?'

The girl had stopped abruptly in the middle of the room, obviously taken aback by her father's friendly attitude towards Linda.

'Have you met Karen, Linda?' Richard deliberately reminded his daughter of the social niceties.

As Karen shook back her smooth, dark-blonde hair and crossed the room towards them, Linda smiled at her.

'How do you do? I've heard about you. You're going to be a journalist, aren't you?'

Even as she was speaking she was thinking the girl was quite beautiful. She had that compelling glow that only excitement and extreme youth can bestow.

'How do you do?' the girl replied, looking slightly chastened. 'Yes — I'm going to college in September.'

She turned back to her father. 'That's what I came to tell you about, Dad. Shall we go through to your office?'

'I don't think that's necessary,' her father told her decisively. 'Have a seat here. I'm sure Mrs Gray would like to hear about your plans. She has two daughters of her own. And what's happened to your school uniform?' he went on. 'Don't sixth formers wear it in the last weeks of term?'

'I've got a job!' Karen announced eagerly. 'That's what I came to tell you.

I dashed home and changed into something more suitable when Miss Graham told me I was to go and see the editor at the Milly Herald about this job.'

'More suitable . . . ' Richard drawled. 'I see!' He raised his eyebrows comically as he surveyed the skimpy black skirt that revealed most of his daughter's long golden legs as she so elegantly crossed them. He hoped she'd been interviewed across a desk because the white blouse and scarlet blazer were undoubtedly impeccable.

'You're still going to college in the autumn, though?' he asked in a concerned tone.

'Of course, Dad — I've just been telling Mrs Gray that. This is called job experience. It's for the summer. Isn't it magic? I'm excused school to start right away, too!'

'Today?'

'Tomorrow. Look at this!' She leaned down and took a folded tabloid-sized newspaper out of the black leather satchel at her feet. 'The editor gave me the last edition to study.'

'The Millway Herald!' Linda exclaimed. 'I recognise it — it's my mother's local paper.'

'The Milly Herald.' Karen gave it its nickname. 'It's awful! I just know I can do better than this. I'm really going to shake up this old rag!'

'I'm sure you will,' her father agreed with a touch of dryness that wasn't lost on her.

'Well, I mean to say, Dad — ' she retaliated ' — listen to this.' She started to read:

"Hitherto famous only for our village green and the fact that the Maid of Millway hid some fleeing Cavaliers from Cromwell's army here — sudden and unexpected prominence has come to the village of Millway.

"In our midst are a group of elderly citizens who see it as their duty to protect for posterity the façade of the old coaching inn, The Rose.

"Its removal, to make way for the

clean lines of a block of energy-efficient, modern flats, fills them with disgust. So says Mrs Gwen Moretti, sixty-five, the instigator of the rebellion.''

Linda felt a surge of alarm rise in her and colour flooded her face.

'Did you ever in all your life hear so many clichés?' Karen went on. 'I would never write like that in a million years!'

'Isn't 'in a million years' awfully like one, dear?' her father returned with a twinkle.

'But, Dad, we're only talking! I would never *write* like that. Miss Graham always says we must avoid clichés like the plague.'

Richard roared with laughter.

'I'll bet she didn't say 'like the plague', dear — because that's another one!'

'It's not just that, Dad. This article should have been livened up with photographs of the old folk waving banners. Or, better still, being arrested for obstructing the bulldozers. That would be much more eyecatching!'

Oh, much more! Linda thought hysterically, her blood running cold in her veins.

'Where's the drama?' Karen demanded rhetorically, waving the paper in the air. 'Dad, would you lend me your camera, please? It's a much better one than mine. I'm going to be the best roving reporter the Milly Herald's ever had!'

* * *

'Have you all seen this?' Gwen had the light of battle in her eyes as she waved the Millway Herald at the group gathered in her house. 'Where's the impartial reporting? I sense a sarcastic tone in this article! We'll have to show them!'

'And fancy them publishing our ages, Gwen,' said Agnes sympathetically. 'I think that was an awful cheek.'

Gwen laughed. 'Oh, that was just a wild guess on their part. I didn't tell them my age — I just said I was over twenty-one!'

'And you don't look it by a day!' Colonel Bingham joked gallantly.

'What's next?' asked Jessica Davis, a rather overweight friend.

'Well!' As Gwen's eyes swept round her sitting-room, she wondered how she came to be sitting at one end of it with the attention of six people trained on her. She'd never sought a position of leadership but seemed to be having it thrust upon her.

'I've heard from the Trust and from the Heritage folk — and they're both sending down representatives this week. Our only worry is that the building firm might move the bulldozers in before they get here. Therefore I feel it's essential that two of us are always there,' she went on decisively, then sighed. 'But we're so short of volunteers and it's very wearisome being shut up in that stuffy place for long periods. I wish some young people would take an interest.'

Even as she spoke a thought crossed her mind.

'My granddaughter's boyfriend seemed a very nice young man, and he seemed quite interested in our campaign. I wonder if he would stay up all night with one of us?' she mused. 'I think I'll get his phone number from my daughter and ask him,' she decided.

'Well,' Rodney Bingham said, looking round the group, 'there's only seven of us here today. Another man would certainly even up the numbers.'

'I wonder when those King's Men were hidden here?' Jack mused, looking to Rodney, as an ex-soldier, to produce the answer.

'Marston Moor, 1644!' Rodney announced, puffing out his chest a bit, unable to hide his satisfaction at knowing the answer.

'But what time of year?' Jack pressed.

'Oh, have a heart!' Rodney groaned, getting up and going to search in Gwen's book-shelves. He hated not being able to supply the answer to any given question.

A shout from him interrupted them a moment later. 'Found it! It was on July the second.'

'That's today!' Jack exclaimed, and a strange, cold thrill ran through the company as they gazed at each other in silence.

'Well!' Gwen spoke the words that they were all thinking. 'One of the Maid of Millway's ghostly appearances might well take place on such a week as this, don't you think?'

'Don't put me down for a night duty this week, Gwen,' Miss Ferris begged.

'Don't worry, Helen. I'll do your duty for you. And, anyway, I'm going to phone that young man Fraser . . . '

★ ★ ★

Signor Ranieri smiled across the dinner table at Nicola. Who would have suspected that in just two weeks the English au pair would have settled in so well and become such an asset?

83

Just an hour before, he had been talking to his son, Angelo, on the telephone. Based in Rome with the carabinieri, he frequently phoned to learn how his son was faring.

'How is the English nurse doing, Papa?' he had asked.

'Very well! Her Italian is very good and — ' Giorgio had chuckled ' — when it isn't, it's very charming! I'm surprised that I find her so agreeable,' he elaborated. 'You know, Angelo, how I have to entertain so often in the evening — clients, business associates as well as our friends? It has been so awkward since your mother died.'

'I know,' Angelo had sympathised.

'I was coming to rely more and more on restaurants. I prefer dining at the villa, though, and I find Nicola quite naturally slips into the role of hostess. She is a very willing young person and very intelligent, very well-informed.'

'I wish she wasn't here only for the summer,' Angelo had put in.

'But it is just an experiment, Angelo. If you feel Carlo is safer with a non-Italian . . . perhaps Nicola will know of someone . . .'

Sitting now at the head of the table, Giorgio once more congratulated himself on his insistence that Nicola join him for dinner each evening. It would have been very dull for her otherwise, he reasoned, always in the company of a child.

Her Italian was improving all the time, and she could now chatter away on many subjects to her nearest neighbours, and if the conversation became general and her opinion was asked, she could be amusing as well as decorative.

This evening the guests were two couples from Naples, friends of long standing. Before long, Nicola found herself being asked questions about the British Government, the economy, the Royal Family, which she answered as best she could.

'To put it briefly,' Giorgio intervened,

trying to help her, 'the hair-raising stories in our newspaper about the Royal Family are . . . all fantasy — and the British Government is thinking of following our excellent Italian lead in fighting crime with something more like our carabinieri.'

'And I shall go to England and show them how!' came a deep voice from the doorway.

'*Mio dio!* Angelo!' Giorgio rose in one agitated movement to his feet. 'But you are in Rome!'

'No, Papa, I phoned from Naples.' Angelo embraced his father. 'I was on business there.'

'*Dio!* I thought you were a ghost! Sit down, sit down! Say hello to everyone. I thought you couldn't risk coming here at present?'

Angelo went round the table greeting everyone in the Italian fashion and shook hands with Nicola.

'Delighted,' Nicola said smoothly in the Italian idiom, as though she had never met him before and as though her heart weren't hammering painfully against her ribs.

'So why are you here?' Giorgio asked, subsiding into his chair at last, still looking shaken.

'I wanted to see Carlo,' Angelo said, sitting down in the space made for him beside Nicola and looking straight into her eyes, giving her the distinct impression that it was she, not Carlo, he had come to check on.

It was decided that as he had already had something to eat, he would join them for dessert.

'Now what was this conversation about the United Kingdom that I interrupted?'

Everyone explained, and then Angelo floored Nicola by asking her what she had found was the main difference between England and Italy since coming out.

Her brain had gone numb since his appearance and his proximity was doing nothing to help her gather her wits.

'Well,' she improvised. 'If we leave

out economics and temperaments . . . I'd have to say the climate.' She smiled up at the revolving fan in the ceiling and listened to the hum of the air conditioning. It was a desperately hot night. 'What is the temperature anyway?'

'About one hundred degrees.'

'Wow! I'd say it would be twenty or thirty degrees cooler in London just now and yet another ten degrees colder in Edinburgh.'

'I'd love to be in Scotland right at this minute,' said one of the ladies. 'Lovely and cool.' She wriggled an expanse of bare shoulder expressively.

'Right at this moment, they'll all be pulling on their cardigans,' Nicola told her wryly.

'Ah, cardigans — that ubiquitous British garment!' the other signora laughed merrily.

'And a most useful garment it is,' Nicola defended it stoutly. 'It's probably one of the greatest British inventions.'

The conversation became very lively

then as they all vied with each other to decide which was really the greatest invention, roving from the spinning frame to telephones and television.

'Come now, Nicola, you must give the British credit for something far greater than the cardigan,' Angelo invited.

'Well, my vote goes to — after Lord Cardigan's cardigan — the Duke of Wellington's wellingtons!'

At that everyone fell about laughing and the rest of the evening passed in a spirit of fun and hilarity.

When Giorgio had said goodnight to his guests he came back into the salon where Nicola was gathering up the coffee cups on to a tray.

'Nicola, thank you so much for helping the party along tonight,' he said. 'You are such fun that I think I will keep you here for ever!'

'Where are you going tomorrow?' Angelo asked her.

'Carlo and I are going to Amalfi. I thought it would be fun for him to go by bus,' she said. 'And I also thought the bus would be safer than taking a Ranieri car.'

'Excellent,' Angelo agreed. 'And we cannot make him a prisoner.'

'Oh, no! Just as long as he doesn't get too adventurous! He already gives me heart failure dashing off like a rocket when something takes his fancy.'

'It is exhausting, I know.' Angelo subsided into an easy chair and Nicola sat down in the corner of a long settee.

Her figure-hugging white dress emphasised her youthful slimness and dramatised her dark hair. She had acquired a light tan since coming out, which set off her simple gold jewellery, and she was aware of Angelo's eyes resting admiringly on her. As for her, she found him overwhelmingly handsome, vital and male.

She felt a wave of unspecified alarm when Giorgio excused himself and went out of the room, leaving her alone in his son's disturbingly attractive presence. She hoped he would soon return. But she chatted as calmly as she could to Angelo and listened carefully to his instructions about Carlo's care.

She was thankful when Giorgio returned and she was at last able to say goodnight and go to her room.

Kidnapped!

Nicola and Carlo sat at a café table in the sunshine gazing out over the heat-haze on the water of Amalfi. It was still early but it would be blisteringly hot later.

The pavement underneath the café tables had just been hosed down and yet it had almost dried before Nicola had finished her fresh-lemon drink and Carlo his ice-cream.

It was very pleasant sitting there watching the world go by and she could have enjoyed lingering over her drink. Not so Carlo.

'*Finito!*' he announced triumphantly, dropping his spoon into his empty dish and hopping down from his chair.

'Oh, wait a minute, Carlo,' Nicola said resignedly, and hastily gulped down the last of her lemon. 'Right — where do you want to go next? Shall we go over to the Cathedral square?'

'OK!' Carlo agreed, and they set off.

'Let's go through this little alleyway.' She pointed and took a firm grip of his hand as a traffic policeman obligingly waved them across the busy road. 'I saw some beautiful little painted tiles here I want to buy.'

He waited patiently by her side while she browsed and selected a few souvenirs, never once letting go of her hand.

Now they were in the Piazza Duomo and there was even more to interest them. Lots of the merchandise was laid out in front of the shops to be studied as they passed by.

Nicola would have loved to have gone into the beautiful cathedral, but she doubted if a small boy would appreciate such an excursion.

'I want to go to the beach!' he complained when she had persuaded him to climb some of the cathedral steps and count them.

'I thought we'd just explore here for a

little while, Carlo, and then go home for lunch,' she coaxed, but his chin jutted obstinately.

'No! We are quite near my beach! Can't we go just for a little while?' he wheedled.

He was so appealing! Nicola looked at her watch. It was still early. How on earth was she going to keep him amused for another two hours until the next bus back to the villa?

'All right, Carlo, that's a good idea,' she conceded. 'Just for a little while. I know what we'll do. We'll take a taxi along to Luigi's beach and then we can take the bus all the way home from there. That will be fun, won't it?'

At the beach Carlo quickly befriended another little boy who was searching the waterline for seashells and soon they were totally absorbed.

Nicola heaved a sigh of relief. That would keep him amused for long enough.

Suddenly an amazing object was flying in the sky above and a little behind them. To an adult it was a most marvellous kite but to a small child it could have been Batman or Superman hovering overhead! All eyes turned to it and every youngster there began running towards it, yelling excitedly, pointing.

Then rockets began to explode on either side of the flying figure and showers of colourful stars drifted to earth.

Nicola supposed it must be a saint's day or something when firework displays were greatly favoured along the coast, although they were generally reserved for night-time.

As she looked round to see how he was enjoying the spectacle, she suddenly realised she could no longer see Carlo.

'Carlo!' she screamed, and instinctively leapt into the crush of children, fighting to catch sight of his head.

At last she reached him and hauled him clear of the crowd.

'You must never, never run away

from me like that!' she scolded him breathlessly.

For a moment she held him tight in her arms, relief giving a certain desperation to her grasp until Carlo began to struggle and she set him down.

'I think we've had enough excitement for one day. Let's go home now.'

Reluctantly Carlo walked with her to the bus stop.

'*Buon giorno, Carlo*,' a woman's voice said.

Nicola swung round to see a young woman smiling at them, and Carlo was smiling shyly back at her.

'*Scusi*,' the woman said apologetically. 'You don't know me. I am Lucia Franchi — a friend of Angelo, Carlo's father. My husband has the car over there — ' she gestured to the road. 'Can we offer you a lift? We will be passing the Ranieri house. Our car has air conditioning.' The woman laughed. 'It will be much more comfortable than the bus in this heat.'

Nicola hesitated then smiled at her. She seemed a nice person.

'Thank you. It's very kind of you.'

Lucia led them to the car where she opened the rear door for them, then she herself got into the front passenger seat.

'My husband — Marco,' she murmured, indicating the man behind the wheel.

He half turned to offer Nicola his hand. '*Signorina*.'

Nicola noticed that he seemed unusually tense, unlike his wife. Perhaps he didn't want to give them a lift. Perhaps he saw it as an inconvenience.

They set off and Nicola relaxed in her seat. The car was wonderfully cool and comfortable. Carlo leaned against her, his eyelids drooping.

About ten minutes later she recognised the winding road they were on. They were almost home. A shower, a light lunch then a nice peaceful siesta for herself and Carlo.

Shortly afterwards she sat forward abruptly.

97

'Marco! Excuse me, but you've just driven past the Ranieri villa.'

Lucia looked round at her. She was no longer smiling.

'We are not going to the Ranieri villa.'

Something in her voice chilled Nicola to the heart.

'What do you mean?' Nicola could hear her own voice rising. 'Where are you taking us?

'You will soon find out.'

Mercifully Carlo was still asleep. Seething with impotent fury, Nicola kept her arm protectively around him as she tried to take in passing landmarks. None of this countryside was familiar to her, but she could see that the car was climbing all the time. So they were heading up into the mountains.

As the car slowed for a junction, she furtively tried the door handle — but it was locked. Her heart sank. There was no chance of grabbing Carlo and scrambling out of the car.

Away to the left she could see a fire-fighting helicopter scooping up water from the sea and conveying it to a vineyard fire high above a village.

The car progressed erratically, bursts of speed being punctuated by tyre-squealing corner-taking. Nicola's hand slid down the side of the seat cushion, gripping it tightly as they took a particularly sharp bend.

She could feel something at her fingertips — paper, cardboard? With some difficulty she pulled it out and, keeping it concealed in her hand, glanced down. It was a book of matches. She cast a quick look at her captors — for that was what she feared they were and she was furious with herself for having fallen into so simple a trap — but their attention was on the road.

Quickly she slipped the matchbook into her pocket. If she could find a pencil or something else to write with, perhaps she could leave a message.

She was sure they were heading for

one of the higher hamlets. She hadn't forgotten Angelo's warning of the other night to stay away from one particular area.

She heard the tolling of a bell and saw a couple of houses just as the car pulled off the road on to a rough track. A moment later it stopped in the shade of some trees by the entrance to a farmhouse.

Carlo stirred beside her. 'Are we home yet, Nicola?' he asked sleepily.

'Not yet, love,' Nicola murmured. 'We'll be there soon. Just you go back to sleep.'

But Carlo was rapidly reaching full wakefulness. He pulled away from her and sat up to look around him.

'Where are we?' he asked, his eyes wide.

Marco opened his door and got out, leaving Lucia to watch them.

Nicola leaned forward.

'Please let us go,' she appealed urgently. 'I don't know who you are but we haven't done you any harm — and the boy isn't much more than a baby.'

Just for a second she saw a flicker of emotion in Lucia's eyes and she pressed on hopefully, 'Please — I won't even tell anyone about what's happened today — '

But before Lucia could reply, the sound of raised voices reached them from the farmhouse. Nicola couldn't make out all the words, but one man was protesting, while the other — probably Marco — was threatening.

A dog began barking loudly, a large dog judging by the deep-throated sound.

Lucia shifted nervously in her seat. Finally she swung round to glare at them.

'Stay exactly where you are. You have nowhere to run to up here — and there are no police around.'

With that she slammed out of the car and hurried towards the farmhouse.

As soon as she had disappeared, Nicola began to move.

'Quick, Carlo!' She grasped the boy's

hand, drawing him after her as she squeezed between the front seats and opened the driver's door. 'Now run as fast as you can!'

Doubled over, they ran for the outhouses at the far end of the farmyard. Nicola stopped at a small barn.

'In here — we'll play hide and seek.'

They hurled themselves into a pile of straw in a corner and Nicola dragged more straw over them.

'Shh, now, Carlo — we must lie here as quiet as two little mice so that they can't find us.'

They hadn't been hiding long when they heard Marco and Lucia returning to the car. There was silence for a few seconds, then Marco began shouting furiously at his partner, who gave back as good as she got.

Finally Nicola heard Marco say, 'They can't have gone far. Let's go!'

Tyres squealing, engine revving wildly, the car shot out of the yard.

They dared not waste a minute. The

two in the car, once they had recovered from their rage, would very soon realise that Nicola and Carlo had not escaped by road.

As soon as the sound of the car had faded a bit, Nicola leapt up out of the straw, grabbed Carlo's hand and practically dragged him across to the house. They burst through the back door and found themselves in a kitchen.

A big, ginger-coloured dog lay mournfully in one corner, his head on his front paws. A middle-aged man was trying to comfort a weeping woman, probably his wife, but they turned with looks of alarm when the young ones erupted into the room.

Nicola urgently demanded that they ring the police and tried to make them understand that they had been kid-napped.

The woman seemed to grasp what she was saying with more alacrity than the man.

'*Si! Si!* Yes! Yes! In here! Quick! Quick!'

She pushed them through a door into a room that contained a large bed and closed the door behind them.

Poor Carlo, terrified out of his wits by now, threw himself onto the bed and began sobbing loudly. Nicola sat beside him, gently stroking his head and telling him everything would be all right now.

Straining her ears, she was sure she could hear the woman telephoning and felt reassured; and for now they were safely hidden in this room till the police came.

With a relieved sigh, she curled up, cradling Carlo in her arms till his sobbing subsided and they both drifted into a kind of doze.

The sound of the door handle turning roused Nicola. She half-rose, a shaky smile of relief and gratitude on her face to welcome the carabinieri.

To her horror, what met her gaze was not the comforting sight of fawn uniforms — but the figures of their two captors.

A Taped Message

Angelo Ranieri found his father pacing up and down his tiled patio, driven by intolerable strain.

'What is it, Papa? I got your message.'

'Nicola and Carlo did not come back for lunch. Raimondo thought they might be lunching out somewhere and chose not to trouble me. But now Luigi has phoned to say that his beach attendant has found Nicola's beach-bag on one of their deck-chairs.'

Angelo paled, fearing the worst,

'I will go at once.'

'I will come with you!' Giorgio announced, but Angelo laid a staying hand on his arm.

'No, Papa. Someone must stay here. There may be a message. A phone call. From them — or from someone else,' he added ominously.'

'This is all your fault, Angelo!' Giorgio choked, unable to check his emotions for a moment longer. 'Why do you have to hunt criminals? Why could you not be in business like me?'

'Papa, we do not know what has happened yet,' Angelo said reasonably enough but Giorgio gave a mirthless laugh.

'We know! I will pay any ransom, even if it ruins me!'

'It isn't money they want, if it is them,' Angelo said ominously. 'Papa, you will excuse me? I must go to Luigi's and look at what was left on the beach, see if anyone noticed anything unusual down there.'

He reached Luigi's hotel sooner than he should have, had he been driving within the speed limits.

'In here.' Luigi hurried him into his office and showed him the few objects scattered on his desk.

Angelo looked inside the straw tote-bag in which Nicola carried all her own and Carlo's needs for a day out.

Her notefold purse and passport she carried in a little shoulder bag which she still had with her, but here were a small sponge-bag of articles for keeping Carlo smart, tissues, make-up, a ballpoint pen and various other unremarkable items.

Also there, in paper bags emblazoned with the names of the shops, were the souvenirs and postcards she had bought that morning.

Beside the bag, on the desk, lay her sun-hat — and a cassette tape.

Angelo stared at it.

'Luigi, was this tape also lying on the seat?'

'Everything that is here my man brought up from the chair. I thought it all belonged to the signorina. Why? Have you found something?'

'The tape has my name on it!' Angelo pointed out grimly.

He brought disposable gloves out of his pocket and put them on before picking up the tape-case.

'Can you get me a cassette-player,

please? And could you find your beach-attendant so that I might speak to him?'

Sadly Ricardo, the beach-attendant, was not a lot of help. He was quite an elderly fellow who kept the hotel's strip of beach as clean and free from litter as though it was his own living-room floor. The beach had been very crowded because of the pleasant sunshine, so Ricardo had been kept busy all day.

Of course he remembered the signorina and Carlo coming down late in the morning. He had instructions from the *padrone* that they were to be accommodated any time, and he had given the signorina the seat she wanted on the row nearest to the water where she could watch Carlo playing all the time.

People often wandered off, leaving things on their chairs, and came back later. It was only in the late afternoon, when everyone had gone and he was tidying up, that Ricardo had noticed that the signorina had not come back for her things.

'I think someone must have left this tape on the signorina's chair. Did you see any odd people hanging about, Ricardo?'

Ricardo shrugged. 'All sorts of people walk along. The water's edge is not private.'

When Ricardo had gone, Angelo put the tape into Luigi's machine.

Any message at all was better than silence. Communication was vital.

He knew he should now hand over the investigation to his colleagues. They were repeatedly warned against emotional involvement. It was forbidden.

But he didn't want to alert his boss just yet. If this was, as he feared, a kidnapping, he dreaded any heavy-handed approach, like a siege of the place where Carlo was being held when they found it. Kidnappers were nervous; the least sign of a raid — and they would kill.

He would give himself one day to see what he could achieve on his own. Tomorrow he would alert his boss.

He pressed the play button on the cassette player and a male voice filled the room.

'Listen! We're taking your son. You know why. You'll find a tape under the seat at the door of your father's garden. It will tell you what to do.'

The colour drained from Angelo's face. So now there was no doubt. Carlo — and Nicola — had been kidnapped.

He put the tape in an envelope borrowed from the desk and began to gather up Nicola's things.

Luigi took one look at his pallor and the attempt to control the tremor of his hands and poured out some brandy.

'Time to call your friends?' he suggested softly, pressing the glass into Angelo's hands.

'Soon, Luigi, soon, I will . . .'

★ ★ ★

After collecting the tape from the bottom of the garden, Angelo hurried into the villa.

110

Giorgio met him in the hall looking even more distraught.

'No phone call, Angelo!'

'No, Papa. But I have a tape here.' He hurried past his father to insert it in the tape player in the living-room.

Giorgio strode up and down, up and down, unable to keep still, head cocked to listen.

'Call off your men, Angelo Ranieri.' It was the same man who had spoken on the previous tape. 'Don't think we don't know who they are. If you cause us any more trouble you will not see your son again. If our goods continue on their way uninterrupted in the future — you may have your son returned to you at a time and a place we will decide. You understand?'

Giorgio sank on to the settee, put his head in his hands and wept, and it was that, probably more than anything, that unnerved Angelo. It seemed to bring home the true horror of the situation.

He was switching off the machine when Giorgio had a fresh thought.

'*Oh, mio dio!*' he gasped. 'We will have to inform Nicola's poor mother! And have you alerted the carabinieri?'

'Not yet, Papa. I'm afraid they may panic the kidnappers into . . . ' He couldn't finish the sentence. 'But I have another idea of who could help us. Teresa used to be a colleague,' he went on. 'She's the best. She left us to set up her own business.'

He looked at his father appealingly.

'Papa, please do not notify Nicola's mother tonight. It might get into the English papers and ruin everything.'

He got out a notebook and searched for a number as he went to the phone.

Teresa was cunning, secretive, highly observant, and brilliant at her job. She had already earned a reputation for tracking kidnap victims and was known to have freed at least two.

But as he reached the phone, a thought occurred to him and he took a step back towards his father.

'Papa — may I hire this woman, in your name? The force had better not know I did this.'

'Of course ... of course. Do anything.' Giorgio raised a tear-stained face. 'Only bring those children home!'

'Yes, Papa.' Eyes showing the strain, making a huge effort to straighten his shoulders, Angelo picked up the phone.

★   ★   ★

Linda felt unaccountably restless. She'd had one of those nights when she couldn't sleep, neither could she get Nicola out of her thoughts. All night her mind had raced round her concerns for her family.

Steve was showing signs of getting depressed owing to the cut-backs and the uncertainty surrounding his job. Gail was doing very well but she was having to count the pennies now that the family's income had been so drastically reduced. Emma was still delicate, while over-sensitive Christopher, only five years old yet picking

113

up on all the anxieties around him, was behaving badly.

Linda's thoughts had hopped over to her mother's latest concern — saving The Rose from the demolition men. Thank goodness that was a fairly harmless preoccupation that would keep her happily busy. At least she could stop worrying about her!

If only Nicola was home! She missed her. Nicola had a naturally happy disposition and wherever she was there was always laughter and fun.

In exasperation at being unable to halt the restless roaming of her mind, Linda had finally thrown back the covers, got up, made herself a cup of tea, and spent the rest of the night reading.

So she was looking pale but outwardly composed as she settled thankfully into her office seat the next morning, telling herself she had no reason to be jumping at shadows.

In contrast, Richard Mason came breezing into the office in excellent spirits and asked her if she would come through to his room and take down a few letters.

Linda gathered up her notepad and followed him, grateful for the distraction.

They were soon immersed in business. Richard was excited about the possibility of a big order and Linda caught his enthusiasm.

He liked to pace about when he was thinking and she kept glancing up at him as she took down his dictation. He was tall, not strictly handsome but attractive with those honest blue eyes.

He was intent on securing this order from a firm in the north.

'I'll have to go up there this week to see them. They still need a little bit of persuasion.'

She took down a letter confirming the date for his visit.

An electronics engineer, he had invented a way of making a vital component in a plastic material instead of metal. This had the potential to save manufacturers huge sums of money, obviously a top concern with them.

His eyes sparkled with the light of enterprise and he dictated several more letters pointing out the advantages of his product to other manufacturers.

When he had finished he sat down behind the desk with a sigh of satisfaction and looked at her, and his very straight, firm mouth broke into a smile.

Her answering smile lit up her face and as he looked at her again, his intent stare made her pulses quicken and a pretty flush rise into her cheeks.

She rose hastily. She felt tremulous but she mustn't let him see that.

'How are you today, Linda?' he asked simply.

'Fine, thank you!'

'I thought you looked a bit pale.'

'Oh, I'm fine. I just had one of those ridiculous nights when you just can't sleep,' she admitted.

He grimaced sympathetically. 'Say no more. I know them well. It's funny how the smallest anxieties can seem insurmountable in the wee small hours.'

She laughed with him, feeling her mood lightening.

'You're right. And when you're a mother, you're never short of something to fret over.'

She tapped her pencil on her notebook. 'I'd better get these letters done. You'll want them to go out today.'

'And then,' he said, his eyes sparkling with fun, 'I know a perfect cure for a sleepless night. We're going out for lunch!'

He took her to a place called The Pen which was cosy and busy with chattering lunch-timers.

He brought her a concoction he'd had the barman make. Its main ingredient was tomato juice but it also contained some magic that made her feel quite human again, and she found she was glad she had let him persuade her about lunch.

'I feel much better,' she told him gratefully.

'Better enough for a bite to eat? That's the next part of the cure. And then do you want to take the afternoon off and go home to sleep?'

'There is nothing,' she declared emphatically, 'that I'd hate more. Tell me how Karen is getting on at the newspaper.'

★ ★ ★

There was a rumour going around that the ghost of the Maid of Millway had been seen again at The Rose.

Nobody knew who had started the rumour. Nobody knew who had seen the ghost. It, or she, hadn't been seen since a fire-watcher, on duty in The Rose during the war, had had a sighting.

'What would she look like?' Gwen asked Colonel Bingham when they were talking about it. 'I wonder what that fire-watcher actually saw?'

'He could tell you,' Rod replied unexpectedly. 'I know him. I see him in the Brewers' Arms quite often. He's a big burly farm-worker.'

Gwen's attractive face flushed with anticipation.

'Could I meet him? He must be very old — the fire-watchers were people who were too old to make the forces.'

'It wasn't always because of age, though. This fellow told me he was pronounced medically unfit, although being in agriculture would have kept him out anyway, I suppose.'

Gwen enjoyed being driven in Rod's car to The Brewers' Arms. It was nice being escorted by a man again.

She was introduced to Bob, who was huge and strong-looking with a thick head of grizzled hair and a healthy complexion. She was astonished when he told her that he had been found medically unfit because, as a child, he had been subject to migraines. He had only been eighteen when he was fire-watching, so was now about the age of many war veterans.

'What did she look like, the ghost of

the maid at The Rose?' she asked him eagerly. 'Do you remember?'

'I remember,' he said in a slow, gruff voice. 'I was upstairs. We was always on the look-out for incendiaries through the roof, y'see.'

Gwen nodded.

'What was she wearing?'

'Hard to say. She wasn't much more than an outline. But maybe a long grey frock? There wasn't much light except a queer glow about her.'

'And what did she do? Did she speak?'

Bob shook his head. 'No sound. She seemed sad somehow.'

'And then what?'

'Then a fire started up the street and I ran to the window and when I turned back she was gone.'

'And just one last question . . . ' Gwen paused. She had seen Fraser come in. She had phoned earlier and asked him to meet her there.

He waved to them and went to get himself something from the bar, and

Gwen turned back to Bob.

'One last question — why do you think it's being said that the Maid is appearing just now?'

Bob scratched his head in thought.

'I dunno. P'raps it's because there's talk of her building being pulled down . . . '

When Fraser came over Gwen introduced him to Bob and began to explain to Fraser why she had asked him to come.

As she spoke, two men and a young girl entered and went up to the bar. The girl was so attractive that most heads turned to look at her.

'Some of the Millway Herald staff,' Rodney whispered.

The barman wanted to know if the young lady, who looked like a school-girl, was under age.

'Of course I am,' she told him cheerfully. 'But I only want mineral water.'

'Ice and lemon?' The barman, completely captivated, smiled at her as she climbed on to a bar stool.

Karen was trying to pick up some of the tricks of the trade from the two reporters.

'Keep your ear to the ground. Have a lot of friends,' said one of the men.

'Eavesdrop?' Karen asked.

'Eavesdropping is essential. Knowing who people are. Being interested. Looking around this room, for instance — there's big Bob Renton who saw the ghost at The Rose during the war. And those are some of the elderly protesters with him — probably asking him about it.'

Karen could hardly contain her excitement.

'I want to get in on that,' she announced. 'But how am I going to manage it?' She thought for a moment. 'Who's the young man with them?'

'I don't know him,' answered the other reporter. 'He's not from Millway, though he looks familiar. He's probably out from town.'

Like so many old villages, Millway

was now more like a suburb of Fieldbridge.

Karen's mind was racing. She had to get her story somehow, but she had decided she didn't want to say too much about her plans to the others. She was sure she could make it a good story and she didn't want them poaching it from her.

Just then Fraser came up to the bar to get a second pineapple juice for Gwen and Karen saw her chance. Turning casually, she deliberately knocked his arm as he lifted the glass, managing to spill some of the juice down the leg of her cream cord jeans.

Fraser was profuse in his apologies, although it wasn't his fault, but she laughed gaily, introduced herself, and quite naturally took the conversation on from there.

*　*　*

Linda was slotting letters into envelopes when the office phone rang. She heard

123

Angelo introducing himself and turned ashen.

'Something's happened to Nicola, hasn't it?' she whispered. 'I knew it!'

'She is not injured, Mrs Gray.' Angelo tried to sound reassuring. 'But — she has been kidnapped, along with Carlo, and they are being held captive.'

Richard came into the office then and saw Linda's anguished face. He went to her side and put his arm round her shoulders. She was aware of it and of drawing emotional strength from him as Angelo's voice went on.

'Mrs Gray, it is very important that no news of this kidnapping leaks out,' he said emphatically. 'Please, I must ask you, do not tell anyone.'

'All right. But I must come out there!' She finished speaking to Angelo and hung up, then briefly explained to Richard what had happened.

'I had to tell you, Richard, but apparently there's a real danger to them if it gets into the news so please, don't say anything to anyone,' she appealed.

'I'm not even going to alert Gail and Steve or my mother . . . at least, not yet.' She shivered, and her eyes were haunted. 'Do you know, even on the day she left, something told me that this trip of Nicola's was ill-starred.'

'Linda, my dear!' He squeezed her shoulder with concern and sympathy. 'Go out there. I'll come with you.'

'Oh, Richard, what a kind offer!' She fought a weak desire to cling to him, and stepped back to break the connection between them. 'But you mustn't risk losing the chance of that new business in the north. No.' She shook her head. 'I'll go alone.'

'People,' he said, looking down into her troubled face, 'come before profits.'

Only One Chance

Since she had received Angelo's phone call, Linda's stomach had not ceased to churn for one second. She could barely control the tremor in her limbs as they finally landed at Naples.

Her forehead felt clammy and her head ached with the effort of trying to appear in control, handle the formalities, and prepare herself to confront the Ranieri family, whom she wanted to blame for allowing this dreadful thing to happen.

Vainly she tried to dispel the thoughts that were hammering at her brain. She had managed to persuade Richard not to accompany her, but she wished now that he had insisted.

Giorgio had driven to the airport to meet her. He wasn't sure if he was fit to be driving, but, while he knew he couldn't have concentrated at the office, the inaction at home had been intolerable.

Linda had little trouble in picking him out. She had been nursing her anger against the Ranieri family, but when she saw the anguish in his brown eyes, her heart went out to him.

'Signora Gray?' Giorgio took her hand in both of his. 'I am so sorry — such a terrible thing to happen. Believe me when I say we will do everything in our power to get your daughter back safely.'

'Signor Ranieri, I wish I had never let her come to your country! Who are these people? And why should they want to kidnap my daughter?'

'Ah . . . ' Giorgio sighed. 'It is my belief that they did not want Nicola at all . . . but she is so good, so brave, so — so dedicated to my grandson, that they could not take him without taking her.'

'If anything happens to her — ' Linda broke off and fumbled for a tissue to wipe her eyes.

Giorgio patted her hand reassuringly. 'Nothing will happen to her. We must make sure of that. Now come, Signora Gray — I shall try to explain everything as we drive to my home.'

As they drove back to the villa, Giorgio told her about Angelo and his job with the carabinieri.

Linda felt her anger growing again.

'Signor Ranieri, if you knew there was danger, why on earth did you employ a young, innocent girl like my daughter?'

Although their conversation had started in English, Linda found herself slipping into Italian. She wanted him to be in no doubt about her feelings. This way there would be no misunderstandings.

'I swear to you that when I hired Nicola I did not know she would be in danger.' Giorgio groaned. 'I have told Angelo that he must give up his work and come into business with me. I could not bear anything like this to happen again! Not only has he put

Nicola at risk but also my own grandchild.' He paused briefly. 'Do you have grandchildren, Signora Gray?'

'I have two — a boy and a girl.'

'And you adore them?'

'Of course!'

'Then you must understand how I feel.'

'Yes . . . yes, I do understand.'

There was no doubting the depth of the man's distress and she could hardly blame him for what had happened. They were in the same dire predicament, and there was nothing to be gained by bickering. Perhaps, instead, they could give each other support and strength.

When they reached the drive of the villa, they exchanged a look that reflected their anguish. Giorgio stretched out his hand and squeezed hers with a wealth of understanding.

'Welcome to my home. I am only sorry it has to be in such difficult circumstances.'

When they were finally in the lounge,

she accepted a seat, controlling her urge to move about the room. Striding up and down, up and down, seemed to be Giorgio's prerogative.

Raimondo came, like a pale ghost, to summon them to the table. He alone of the household was trying to order things in the normal way while dealing with Maria and Anna, who were punctuating their tasks with fits of hysterical weeping.

'Come, we must keep up our strength,' Giorgio insisted.

Linda's stomach was twisted so tight that she doubted if she could manage any food, and her mouth was as dry as cement. She wondered if some of Giorgio's wine might even have a welcome, calming effect on her, but the pain in her heart was beyond the reach of wine.

★ ★ ★

Nicola and Carlo were in a room above a stable, deep in a desolate stretch of countryside. They might as well have been in the middle of an ocean, Nicola thought. Hill after hill, covered with vegetation, rolled away on all sides.

It was the middle of the night. Two-thirty in the morning — and dark. Nicola knew with certainty that if they were ever going to make a bid to escape it had to be now.

The stable-loft was built of wood, thin streaks of light showing between the planks in the day-time. There were no windows and only a low door in the gable-end which led out on to steps.

There was always a guard out there. One was there right now. From the sound of the snoring, she guessed it was the woman.

Nicola pulled the empty match-book she'd found in the car out of her pocket. Tumbling in her mind were thoughts of scratching some message on it and posting it out of one of the cracks in the wood. It might not be noticed in the general way — but a good detective could easily take note of

131

it, if one ever came that way. She'd gathered that this was only a temporary stop for her and Carlo.

However, when she opened the little gold of cardboard her heart leapt. Unbelievably, miraculously, two of the tiny matches were still clinging inside!

Her mind raced as she looked round the loft. It was empty except for the threadbare straw pallet on which they lay.

While Carlo continued to sleep heavily, Nicola began quietly widening the splits in the mattress-cover and teasing out the stuffing.

In a quarter of an hour she had a stack of musty straw piled in front of her. Then she froze, her heart lurching, as a donkey brayed somewhere nearby, giving the cockerel the notion of outdoing him. The snoring outside the door stopped abruptly as the guard awakened. However, the noises were followed by silence once again and the guard was soon asleep and snoring once more.

Finally Nicola woke Carlo and whispered to him what she planned to do. Then she told him all over again. It was essential that the poor mite understood exactly.

Gradually he became more alert, but he clung to her as he had been doing lately. She hugged him reassuringly, praising and encouraging him.

'You're super to be with, Carlo!' she told him. 'Brave and clever, just like your dad! He'll be so proud of you! We'll do it! It's worth a try, anyway!' She spoke to him as though he were a grown-up.

'But I'm scared, Nicola!' he whispered tearfully.

'I'll tell you a secret — so am I!'

She knew she was taking a desperate chance of incinerating them — but she was gambling against a far worse fate.

Nicola pushed her straw stack over closer to the door, dragging the remains of the bedding after it and arranging it just behind.

Then, with hope in her heart, she

struck the first match.

In consternation she saw that first match fizzle out.

Near despair, shaking with apprehension, she tried the other one — the last one.

It flared feebly — but for long enough to ignite the torn card which she held to it, then pushed under the loose straw.

She waited till the straw had caught and there was no doubt that the fire was going, then banged urgently on the door.

'Help!' she yelled. 'Fire — the room is on fire!'

Carlo added realism by wailing with terror and she gave him a quick thumbs-up of encouragement.

'What is it?' a sleepy voice grumbled from outside. As Nicola had suspected, it was the woman.

'Fire! Fire!' Nicola yelled urgently.

The woman cursed, but smoke was beginning to billow under the door now and she couldn't ignore it.

Finally Nicola heard the heavy bolt being moved, and she drew Carlo over beside her, behind the door.

The door creaked open and the woman appeared.

She gaped at the pile of straw, now well alight, and seizing that moment of stunned inactivity, Nicola leapt out and pushed her with both hands. As the woman staggered forward and fell, Nicola grabbed Carlo by the hand and raced with him down the steps.

As they fled into the night, they heard the spluttered, '*Mama mia!*' before smoke, followed by flames, billowed out of the door and the woman's piercing shrieks curdled the air. A man shouted hoarsely as he went to her aid.

The darkness was their saviour as they ran, stumbling, into the surrounding wilderness of shrubs and trees. It was the vital element in their escape as the dry wooden building that had been their prison burst into flames and demented activity exploded all around it.

The donkeys were braying loudly and the cockerel sounding his alarm.

As they ran blindly, deep into the trees, ears pricked for the crash of following footsteps, they instinctively ducked as they heard a huge explosion come from behind them.

Something from the blaze must have fallen into fuel, Nicola guessed. Perhaps even into the kidnappers' car, she thought hopefully. Everything, anything that would dismay and delay their captors was welcome.

She had no idea which way they were running as, heedless of whipping branches and scratches from the undergrowth, she dragged Carlo through the forest.

★　★　★

Angelo had barely slept since he'd been alerted to the kidnap. He and Teresa, the private detective he had engaged, had, on the pretence of being honeymooners with an interest in folk-lore, followed a very slender lead and had now reached the farm from which, although they didn't know it, Nicola and Carlo had first tried to escape.

Sensing something furtive about the farmer, they hung around.

'It's lovely scenery. Do you get many strangers coming up here to appreciate it?' Angelo asked him casually.

'There's a rumour going about that a woman and a boy have gone missing somewhere in this area,' Teresa murmured in a disinterested manner.

'Oh, these reports are always nonsense, *cara mia*,' Angelo scolded her lovingly, but he didn't miss the look that passed over the man's face. Guilt was written all over him.

However, short of revealing his own identity in order to arrest him, frustratingly there was nothing Angelo could do at that moment to get at the truth.

Reluctantly they went back to their car, but then, by pretending that they couldn't get the vehicle to start, they manufactured the excuse to ask their suspect for a room for the night.

With an ill-concealed reluctance that reinforced their feeling that they were on the right track, the man agreed.

At least it gave them a chance to try to investigate further.

While Teresa caught forty winks, Angelo paced the room, fretting.

Finally he left the room and climbed the hill, peering hopelessly all around in the darkness, trying to discern any tracks that might lead to other habitations.

He thought he saw one which, in the morning, with the car miraculously restored to health, they might follow.

It was then that he noticed a light springing up several miles away to the east.

He watched it curiously for some time, until he decided that it was a fire — and not a small one either. He wondered if there were people living up there and if they had any way of alerting the emergency services. It seemed most unlikely. And it was the devil of a place to reach.

He set off in the direction of the flames. He had his phone with him and could alert the services if he identified any need.

It was action, at least, something with which to distract himself from the anguish he was living with. It beat lying on a bed trying to sleep.

He couldn't explain it to himself, either, but he was experiencing a strong sensation that the fire had some connection with his quest. It was drawing him on. He had to investigate it.

★　★　★

Richard Mason drove north with mixed emotions. The business he hoped to complete would normally have absorbed his mind but at present his thoughts were with Linda.

He was identifying with her, imagining the cold horror he would be experiencing if it were Karen who had

139

been kidnapped.

The feeling of being powerless to help was almost more than he could bear. He longed to fold Linda in his arms and somehow soothe away all her agony. He knew he should have gone with her.

A car that he hadn't even registered gaining on him, suddenly whipped past with a woosh and, momentarily startled, he shook himself out of his daydreaming, forcing himself to concentrate wholly on the road.

In his hotel bedroom in Newcastle he had a strong desire to telephone Linda in Italy, to find out how things were progressing. He even got as far as picking up the phone. But then, he thought, perhaps better not. She would soon let him know if there was any good news. And, if there wasn't, it would only add to her distress to have to talk about it.

With a sigh he hung up and stared unseeingly out of the window. At least here he was safe from the possibility of meeting any of Linda's family and having to lie about her whereabouts.

Being deliberately vague, she had left word that suggested she had come with him on this business trip, and as long as he didn't appear without her, it would hold water.

It was hard keeping the knowledge of Nicola's kidnap to himself. His mind consumed with worry about her, he had had to make a huge effort not to reveal his concern to Karen the night before.

'Dad! What's wrong with you? I don't think you've heard one word I've been saying!' she'd complained.

'Mmm? Sorry — what was that, darling?'

'I said I'd met Linda's mother, Mrs Moretti. She's leading the campaign to preserve that old building in Millway.'

Oh, no! Richard had thought. What's it going to do to her grandmother, let alone the others, if Nicola . . . ?

Karen had chatted on excitedly.

'Then there's this young guy, Fraser Blyth, who's helping. He's a lot of fun

— a lot more mature than the boys in my crowd. He gave me a lift home on his motor-bike.'

That got his attention. It was the kind of information guaranteed to automatically switch on parental concern, and he found himself wishing that her mother was here to help him cope with their teenage daughter.

His mind swerved away from the hopelessness of that thought, but even so, he was conscious now that the nightmares he had suffered since his wife had deserted him were fading.

It was a different sweet face, Linda's face, that now swam in and out of his dreams, obliterating all others.

★ ★ ★

Gail wished her mother would hurry back from her business trip. She needed to talk to her, to ask her advice.

Steve was working only three days a week now, and Gail's friend at the grocer's shop on the estate had offered her work on the days he was at home. He would be able to look after Emma, and Christopher, too, once the school holidays started.

Gail realised that, in addition to easing their financial worries, working outside her home for a while would benefit her. Her nerves were screaming, and she knew she wasn't coping well with Christopher's tantrums. The children would gain from having Steve around instead.

She'd tried to talk it over with Steve, but he was so depressed he was quite unlike himself. He did say, though, that he didn't want her to go out to work, blaming himself for the necessity, not realising how beneficial it would be for her.

'Gail, orders might come in!' he argued. 'We might get a big contract — and we'll all be on full-time again.'

'I know, and I'm sure that could happen, but . . . ' She looked down at the unpaid bills lying on the table. 'Let me put it this way, Steve. I'd really enjoy being out of the house for a spell some days. I mean, knowing that the children were safe and happy with you. Probably happier than with me, because I'm always so cross these days.'

'Because I'm no use!' Steve pushed his chair back roughly, almost tipping it over. 'No use as a husband and no use as a father! You'd all be better off without me. At least you'd have the insurance money and the mortgage would be paid off. And you're so gorgeous, Gail, some other bloke would want to marry you. Someone who would provide properly for you. Not a useless character like me!'

'Stop it, Steve! I won't have you talking like that. We're managing fine! Obviously the money would be useful, but to be honest, I'd give anything to have a change of scene.'

She thought for a moment. Could she come up with any more persuasive arguments?

'I'll tell you what! We'll ask Mum what she thinks. You'd agree to it if

Mum thought it was a good idea, wouldn't you? You trust her judgement.'

'OK,' Steve conceded.

★ ★ ★

Giorgio couldn't help but admire the control and fortitude of Nicola's mother. It must be the English part of her blood that enabled her to appear outwardly calm in the midst of this horror.

He knew she was just as frightened and worried as he was, but she was maintaining a remarkable façade of politeness and appreciation of the efforts of Raimondo, Maria and Anna to make her comfortable.

She never forgot to thank them for little services. She never forgot to force a smile, however strained, for his own, somewhat distracted, small attentions. He only wished they had met in happier circumstances.

He tried to imagine what the behaviour of his late wife or of some of his Italian women friends would have been in a similar scenario. He suspected that tears, hysterics, recriminations and blame would have been flying around.

'What shall we do?' Giorgio stopped his pacing of the patio long enough to ask Linda helplessly. 'We daren't leave the house in case there is some word. If only I could take you and show you Pompeii or Herculaneum or Paestum, it would be better. I wish you were here on holiday. We could go to Capri and Ischia! But how can we even leave the house? Yet the inaction is making everything worse. It is killing us!'

'I know what you mean,' Linda agreed.

She looked around at the cascading bougainvillaea, at the huge pots of dazzling geraniums, at the grape vines growing over the patio. It certainly would be a glorious place for a holiday.

'It must be like this when people you love are at war,' she mused. 'You feel you shouldn't do anything but remain in a kind of vigil, keeping them constantly in your thoughts, never ceasing to cover them with prayer. You're scared that if you let your concentration go for a moment, some harm may come to them.'

He stared at her in amazement. Then he dragged a chair in front of hers and took her two hands in his and gazed deep into her eyes in wonder.

'That's it! That's it exactly!' he exclaimed. 'I've never met anyone like you! Is that what you have been doing?'

'Yes,' she whispered.

'Why are you so wonderful?' He smiled at her. 'I've needed to meet someone like you for a long time. I've always been the macho man . . . we Italians like to be that! But now I ask your advice . . . What shall we do?'

'Well . . . ' Linda gave the question deep thought. 'If we go on the way we have been doing for many more days, I think there's a real danger that we'll make ourselves ill. Perhaps we should try to have a more optimistic attitude.'

'But I'm afraid to hope,' he interrupted despairingly. 'I'm afraid to hope in case the outcome is all the more terrible in the end!'

Tears filled his eyes and prompted an answering emotion in Linda.

However, she made an immense effort not to collapse though the temptation was almost irresistible. She would be put to bed by the kind girls and given a sedative. She could drift away into oblivion. The unbearable pain would recede.

Oh, how she coveted oblivion! But that wouldn't help Nicola or Carlo, nor would it help Giorgio and Angelo.

She swallowed over the huge lump in her throat, hoping her voice wouldn't let her down.

'I imagine you have a mobile phone?'

'Yes, yes, of course.'

'So Raimondo can reach you if you are away from the house?'

'Of course!'

'What is Angelo doing?'

'Everything that can be done.'

'And what are we doing?'

'Going crazy?' His laughter held a note of despair. 'Come on — let's speak to Raimondo!' He pulled her out of the chair. 'I can show you a beautiful church where we can pray just as well, maybe better, than we can here.'

'Safe Now . . . '

When Carlo was plainly exhausted and Nicola knew she couldn't take another step, they collapsed on the ground. There had been no sound of pursuit.

It might have been for hours that they just lay there, panting and shivering, waiting for the agony in their lungs to ease.

When they had recovered sufficiently to move a little, they crawled farther into the screening undergrowth and, totally hidden, drifted in and out of uneasy, listening sleep for the remainder of the night.

Fingers of sunlight and the distant drone of a helicopter teased them awake.

The memory of what had happened at the first farm they had been taken to was still so sharp in Nicola's mind that she knew she wouldn't dare approach any house around here. What if the gang who had kidnapped them held the whole area in fear?

What troubled her most, however, was the awareness that they had run very far inland and there seemed to be nothing but endless hills around them. How terrible if she couldn't find a way out and, after all they had been through, they perished of starvation and exhaustion.

Well, she told herself, the sun is rising in the east, so if we head in the opposite direction, we'll surely come to the coast.

But what if they found themselves walking right into the path of the kidnappers?

After a long debate with herself, she decided to take what she hoped was a northerly direction. At least they could see now where they were putting their feet.

They walked for a while until they came upon a shallow stream. With a glad cry Nicola sank to her knees and helped Carlo to drink some water out of her cupped hands. Then she sipped some herself, knowing that no champagne could have tasted better at that moment.

Carlo was staggering and whimpering with fatigue. She tried to carry him for a while, but he was too heavy for her to manage that for long. All she could do was place him back on his feet and slow down their pace to barely a crawl.

After some hours had passed she realised that although they were still amongst trees, they were now walking on a narrow but clearly defined track.

The heat had grown more intense as the sun rose in the sky, and finally it got so fierce that she knew they would have to rest, perhaps even until the evening.

She searched for a hollow, one well screened by vegetation, where they might lie hidden for a while. Finally they found just what she sought and collapsed once more on to the hard ground.

Carlo, curled within the curve of her

body, slept, but she found it harder to relax, worrying about the evening hours when they must resume their journey. In the darkness it was so easy to lose one's bearings and get lost.

She could have sworn she hadn't slept when terror seized her. She was staring up into the wolf-like muzzle of a large dog!

Rigid with fright, Nicola held her breath as the dog panted over them. She clutched Carlo tightly, feeling her temples beginning to pound.

She could hear heavy footsteps crashing through the undergrowth towards them.

'Bruno!' A deep voice called to the dog, and suddenly Nicola was a child again, asleep in her grandmother's garden, with her grandfather calling.

That well-loved, deep familiar voice would call, '*Nicolina! Cara mia!*' and call his dog, Bruno, to heel . . .

The footsteps stopped, and the man was standing over them, staring down in surprise.

'*Dio!*'

His face was not unlike Grandpa's, but she saw that he was taller and younger. He must be in his sixties.

He pushed the dog's head aside, his hand cupped over its nose, and hunkered down beside them.

Carlo was awake, his head pressed hard against Nicola's shoulder as he gazed at the stranger.

'Who are you? Are you lost?' the man asked in Italian.

Was it safe to tell him? Her instinct was to confide in him, but might even this seemingly trustworthy person return them to the gang?

He didn't seem to know that a small boy and his nanny were missing, and dazed though she was, Nicola's heart sank at the thought. Angelo must be trying to avoid publicity. They were still in danger . . .

Nicola shivered and the man frowned in concern.

'You are weak. Hungry?'

She nodded, and he stretched out his

arms to take Carlo. To her astonishment, given all that he had been through, the little boy allowed himself to be lifted. If Carlo instinctively trusted him . . .

The man seemed a very ordinary countryman, dressed in old trousers and a brown checked shirt. He was smiling at the boy, a smile that transformed his face. He must have been stunning in his youth, Nicola thought disjointedly.

She scrambled to her feet, and nearly fell as faintness and sickness swept over her.

'Home, Bruno!' The man had turned away, and Nicola struggled to regain her balance and follow him. Tears of weakness filled her eyes, and she longed to lean on this stranger who so reminded her of the familiar strength and security of her grandfather.

She had to stop for a moment, bending over until the blood returned to her head, and he waited for her calmly, talking quietly to Carlo about the dog and the birds they could hear singing.

They followed the woodland path for a while, then skirted fields before threading their way through a vineyard.

She saw a group of buildings ahead. There were no roads, only alleyways between the houses, but with a shock, she realised the danger.

'We mustn't be seen!' she broke out urgently, in English, and the man looked at her in surprise.

'You are not Italian!' he exclaimed. 'You looked like an Italian girl. But the *bambino*!' He studied Carlo with the gentle adoration of an Italian for his child. 'He's too beautiful to be anything but Italian!'

Nicola managed a weak smile.

'We mustn't be seen,' she repeated desperately, and he recognised the urgency in her voice.

He nodded. 'This way.'

He led them along a quiet alleyway at the back of the houses, and in through a doorway. Bruno remained outside, spreading himself across the entrance.

A neat little woman about the same age as the man looked round in surprise from the stove.

'*Mama mia!*'

With Carlo sound asleep on his shoulder, the man began to explain where he had found them.

'*Proverino!*' The woman left her cooking and came over to examine Carlo's angelic little face. 'Straight from heaven!' she breathed, turning to Nicola and smiling.

She gestured to a seat, and Nicola sank thankfully into it.

'You are English. He is not your son,' the woman said.

'They must have food and rest first, Marta,' her husband told her. 'Then questions.'

He lowered Carlo carefully on to a padded bench.

'You are safe now for a while, *caro*,' he said tenderly, and suddenly the truth of that hit Nicola.

Sure she was going to faint with

relief, she sank into a chair by the table and rested her head on her arms as she listened to the quiet, comfortingly normal sounds around her.

Soon her arm was gently touched, and Marta placed a dish of food in front of her.

Nicola astonished herself by eating a bowlful of the pasta, washed down with water with some wine in it.

When she'd finished, she was overcome by a weariness so total that it couldn't be hidden. With a sympathetic smile the woman took her to what was obviously their own bedroom.

Gratefully Nicola collapsed on to the bed, only managing to say, '*Grazie,*' before pitching fathoms deep into sleep.

* * *

Running steadily towards the blaze, Angelo used his mobile phone to call the fire service. The helicopter should get there soon after he did, he reckoned.

The place was well alight. Though he was desperate to rush forward and help the men who were futilely throwing buckets of water at the flames, he held back. Blowing his cover now would be useless — and, for Carlo and Nicola, dangerous. Somehow he was sure that this place held some connection with them.

He hid behind a wall, listening hard to the few words that emerged from the din and confusion.

'We can't save the buildings! Go after them! They can't have gone far!'

It had to be Nicola the man meant — Nicola, clinging bravely to his darling son . . .

Torment held Angelo motionless for what seemed like eternity. Then he shook his head to clear it. If this was where they had been held captive, at least they had got out. Perhaps Nicola had even engineered this as a distraction.

If only he knew which way they had run!

There was a point beyond fear, and Angelo reached it then. He knew the time had come to call in his colleagues.

He phoned Teresa. Her answer came in a quiet voice as she surfaced immediately, totally, from sleep.

'Yes?'

'Angelo.'

'What?' Her voice was low, but urgent. 'Have you found the trail?'

'I think so.'

He explained what was happening.

'Where are you?' she asked.

He described the location as best he could.

'Call the force for me, Teresa. They can follow the fire helicopter. Tell them everything — they can sack me if they want, as long as they find Carlo.'

'Leave it to me.'

She was a wonderful woman. Few words, straight into action.

Lying behind his wall, Angelo had nothing to do but fret. If these people were who he guessed they were — the kidnappers in the employ of the big boys — and he confronted them now, they would have no choice but to kill him.

Distracted by the fire, the gang at first greeted the fire-fighting helicopter with amazed relief. It flew in low, deluged the flames with tons of sea-water and flew off for another load.

They didn't realise the second helicopter's arrival had nothing to do with the fire until it was too late.

Bent low, Angelo sped to join his colleagues as soon as they landed. The kidnap gang, three men and a woman, seeing the uniforms and guns, took flight in different directions, with the police in pursuit.

After quickly briefing the officer in charge, Angelo was at last free to help in the hunt for his son — and Nicola.

★ ★ ★

Giorgio and Linda, distracted by worry, had driven down to St Andrew's Cathedral in Amalfi.

The colourful cathedral dominated the square. They climbed the immense flight of steps to the welcome dimness of the triple-arched porch, and went through the great bronze doors to the cool interior.

They sat there for a while, drinking in the peace. Linda found it hard to pray at first. With every breath she drew, she feared for Nicola. It was not knowing that was the worst. Not knowing where her daughter was, how she was . . .

She closed her eyes, and at last she was able to pray, with a fervency that surprised her.

'Look after her,' she pleaded. 'Take care of my girl — and Giorgio's little grandson . . . please . . . '

Giorgio rose from his knees and crossed the floor to light candles. Through her tears, Linda watched as he bowed his head in prayer.

They didn't speak as they left the church, walking through the cloisters in silence.

Out in the heat the decorated tiles

and terracotta walls shimmered in the intense sunlight.

'This is so unbelievable!' Giorgio burst out. 'How is it that we are walking here in the sunshine while our children are in terrible danger?'

'Don't, Giorgio!' she pleaded, her eyes filling again with the tears she found so hard to banish. 'You know why we're here. We have to pass the time somehow until there's some news.'

He looked away.

'I am so sorry! How could I let this happen to your daughter? I am in torment, Linda.'

'And so am I,' she said quietly.

He looked at her directly.

'You are so pale, Linda . . . and the shadows under your eyes are so dark. And it's all my fault!'

He touched her hand, then folded it into his own. His hand was smooth, reassuring, as it engulfed hers, and in a moment she was in his arms.

He held her close, and she felt herself beginning to relax for the first time since that first phone call with its awful news.

As he cradled her in his arms, she gave a little murmur and rested her head against his shoulder. It felt so good to be held, to be consoled — she needed this so badly . . .

'There, *cara*,' he murmured. 'Lean on me for a while. Let me bear the burden just for a few moments. You are right, we feel the same . . . '

His arms tightened as she moved a little.

'Ssh, I am here. Rest a little.'

She did, and it was wonderful. His sheer physical strength seemed to envelop her, and all of a sudden her courage began to flow back.

She drew away a little at last, and looked into his dark eyes.

'Thank you,' she said simply.

He leaned forward and brushed her forehead with his lips.

'We need some calm.' His voice was husky. 'We make some space for each other amid this terror, Linda.' His voice dropped. 'We go back into the cathedral now, yes? For me, it is all I can do to help Carlo — and Nicola.'

Inside, although for her it was a novel thing to do, she lit a candle for the safety of Nicola and Carlo. The flame burned bravely, and as she let Giorgio draw her to a seat, she felt a faint flutter of hope — the first since she had heard the news.

They watched the candles burning until, mesmerised by the flames, Linda began to experience a measure of peace. Being in this place helped, but so did Giorgio's closeness.

He held his rosary in his fingers, and its smooth motion as he touched each bead, murmuring his prayers, soothed her, too.

'I'd like to stay here for a while,' she whispered to him when his fingers paused. 'It's a comforting place.'

He nodded.

'Shall I leave you? I should see my friend, Luigi. He was there when Angelo played the tape — he will be worrying.'

'Yes. Please. I'd like some time on my own here.'

She felt a slight, unaccountable lightening of her burden, as though a quiet voice was assuring her that everything would be all right.

She realised, in the calmness of the moment, that she must get in touch with Gail, and her mother. She had wanted to spare them, especially Gwen, but if there was no news of Nicola soon, they would have to be told.

★ ★ ★

Gail had butterflies in her tummy as she entered the Lawsons' shop. She was nervous to be starting something new, but she was also excited.

It had been an extraordinary feeling, leaving Steve behind with the children and walking along to the store. She had been let off the leash, and it felt surprisingly, shockingly good.

The family-owned grocery store served the whole estate, and was always busy.

'It's great to see you, Gail!' Moira Lawson greeted her cheerfully. 'We're really short-handed till Rita gets back.'

Gail started the day re-stocking shelves, and later relieved one of the assistants at the delicatessen counter.

'Would you like to go home for lunch, Gail?' Moira asked. 'Or have it here with me in the staff-room?'

'I'd like to stay,' Gail told her. 'I think I might just unsettle the children by appearing and then rushing off again. Steve will have everything under control.'

But she crossed her fingers as she said it.

By the end of the day, Gail felt like a different person. She had mastered everything faster than she had thought possible, and felt she had earned her money.

When she got home, she walked into Steve's arms for the bear hug they always exchanged when he returned from work. But it was a brief, perfunctory embrace she received, and

Steve moved away quickly, to check the potatoes, he said.

'I'll do that!' she called after him, dropping her coat on the hall chair. 'I'll just say hello to the kids first.'

She wanted to pick them up and cuddle them after this long day apart, but they were engrossed in a jigsaw puzzle.

'Hi, Mum,' Christopher said casually, and Emma reached up distractedly for a kiss before getting busy again.

Gail was thoughtful as she went to hang up her coat and wash her hands. Steve was doing almost too well here. She hadn't realised before how much she liked to be in control — at least in her home.

She went to join Steve in the kitchen, looking round futilely for something to do.

'It's all ready,' he said testily.

'I can set the table at least.'

'It's done.'

'Oh, I see. Well? Don't you want to hear how I got on today?' she

168

challenged him brightly.

He had his back to her and didn't even turn to look at her as he obligingly asked, 'How did you get on?'

'Very well . . . ' Gail trailed off. She wanted to tell him all about it, but clearly he wasn't interested.

'I'll just go and make a quick call to Mum,' she said. 'I'll be right back.'

Her mother should be back from that business trip with Richard Mason by now.

However, when there was no reply Gail, feeling slightly worried, tried Richard's home number.

'Karen Mason. Can I help you?' It was a young voice, but self assured.

Gail introduced herself and explained.

'My father's just arrived home,' Karen said. 'Would you like to speak to him?'

She held the phone out to Richard and murmured warningly, 'It's Linda's daughter, Gail, wondering where you've put her mother.'

Richard's heart sank. This was what

169

he had been afraid of when Linda had made her hurried departure. He knew she had been anxious to spare her mother and her elder daughter any worry, but the longer the wait without news from her, the harder it would become for him to keep the secret.

He took the receiver as though it was a live cinder.

'Richard Mason speaking.'

He sounded more distant than he had meant to, and Gail felt embarrassed that she had troubled her mother's boss at home.

'I'm — I'm so sorry to trouble you, Mr Mason,' she stammered. 'I was trying to contact my mother. I understand she was with you on a business trip?'

Richard searched in his mind for a reply that wouldn't betray Linda's trust, and couldn't find one.

'Gail, I think you'll find your mother's gone out to Italy.'

'On business?'

'Er — personal business,' he hedged.

Gail's heart began to race. There was something not right here!

'Can you give me a number?' she asked, anxiety sharpening her tone.

'I'm sorry but she didn't leave me one. I'm sure she'll be in touch with you shortly, Gail.'

Afterwards she couldn't believe that she had thanked him, said goodbye and hung up without asking him any more questions . . .

* * *

Richard groaned as he put the phone down. God forbid that he should ever have to keep someone else's secret again.

'Dad, did I hear you say that Linda's gone to Italy?'

He groaned again. This was all he needed!

'Karen, listen.' He sat down opposite his daughter. 'I want you to set your reporter's instincts aside for a bit. This isn't your business any more than it's

171

mine. All I know is that there's a problem with Nicola, Linda's younger daughter.'

'Why didn't you tell the other one, then?'

'Because I've been sworn to secrecy. Linda doesn't want to worry the family at home.'

Karen looked at him closely.

'Dad, this cloak and dagger scene just isn't you!'

Richard grinned at her.

'Don't I know it! But I couldn't refuse to help Linda — she had to go out there at a moment's notice. And I'll warn you now that I may have to follow her, to give her some support.'

Karen frowned. 'But I thought you had a new order hovering on the horizon?'

'That's true.' Richard gazed into the fire. 'But it may have to wait — if Linda needs me.'

Karen was silent for a moment.

'You like her, don't you?' she ventured.

It was Richard's turn to pause.

'I've never set out to replace your mother, Karen. But there's something about Linda, I must confess.'

He looked up at her, with no idea of the appeal for understanding that shone out of his eyes.

'Do you mind?'

His daughter saw the look in his eyes and suddenly the hard-boiled façade crumbled.

'No, I don't mind, Dad.' She smiled. 'Though I think I might prefer her mother. Mrs Moretti's a real character!'

Karen didn't tell her father that she was just about to go and meet Gwen Moretti, the colonel, and Fraser Blyth.

★ ★ ★

When she met them later at The Brewer's Arms, Gwen's face showed relief.

'Oh, Karen,' she greeted the girl. 'I'm so worried about Linda! I was hoping you'd put my mind at rest.'

Fraser brought over coffee for everyone and joined them.

'Gail's just been on the phone to me.' Gwen held Karen's eyes. 'She says your father told her that Linda has gone to Italy on personal business. But why would she do that without telling me?'

Karen's heart went out to this feisty lady. She had had the guts to take on this fight for The Rose, at her age, and the last thing she needed was to worry about her family.

Suddenly she realised the dilemma her father was in and decided to take the same approach he had, of coming clean.

'I'm afraid it's some problem with Nicola, Mrs Moretti,' she said reluctantly.

Gwen slapped the table with her hand.

'I was afraid of this! What's wrong? Do you know?'

'No, I'm sorry. Linda swore Dad to secrecy — he wasn't even supposed to say where she'd gone.'

Fraser had been talking to the colonel, but Nicola's name had caught his attention.

'Did someone mention Nicola? What's happened?' His face was pale. 'Is she ill?'

'I don't know. I shouldn't even have said this much,' Karen told him.

'If it wasn't for The Rose,' Gwen said, 'I could go out to Italy and be with Linda.'

'I'll go with you, Gwen,' the colonel offered.

'No, let me,' Fraser said. He was still white to the lips. 'Whatever the problem is, I want to bring Nicola home.'

'I'm sure you do, Fraser.' Gwen leaned forward. 'But if I — '

'Dad says he's going,' Karen chipped in. 'He knows his way around, Mrs Moretti. If Linda needs any support, he's the right person to give it.'

Gwen was thinking hard.

'I could phone the Ranieris,' she

suggested. 'I wonder why Gail didn't do that?'

Karen smiled faintly, wishing she had kept her mouth shut.

'Because Dad didn't actually tell her where Linda was. I would leave it for a little while, Mrs Moretti,' she urged. 'Dad's doing all he can and I know he'll keep in touch once he does go out there.'

The colonel came back from the bar just then, carrying drinks.

'No arguments, Gwen.' He handed her a dry sherry. 'You get that inside you. Now, nobody's going off to Italy right away, so why don't we sit down and do what we're here to do, which is to talk to Karen about our campaign to save The Rose?'

He patted Gwen's hand. 'I know how you feel, my dear, but you can't help Nicola or Linda at the moment — and we can do something for The Rose, thanks to Karen . . . '

An Astonishing Discovery

As she awoke, Nicola was bewildered. Where was she? Why was she so tired? And then it all flooded back.

But she felt safe here. Why? She lay for a moment, gazing idly at the walls and ceiling. It was like being in Gran's spare room. What was there that reminded her of Gran and Grandpa?

There it was again, that sense of something familiar, this time a picture on the wall. It was too far away to make out, but something about it reminded her . . .

She closed her eyes again. She was still so very tired . . .

When she woke again, the weariness had gone and the urgency of the situation returned to her in full force.

'Come on,' she said to herself, sitting up cautiously. 'You've got to get a grip on yourself. Where's Carlo? We have to get back to the Ranieri villa.'

She had a shower, such a wonderful shower that she was loath to stop scrubbing and come out of it. After all this she felt as though she would never be clean again.

When she went back into the bedroom, the signora had been in and laid out some clothes for her.

She had also opened the shutters, and for the first time Nicola saw the framed photograph properly.

It was Gran's photo! There were Grandpa and Gran Moretti in their thirties, with Mum and Uncle Paul!

'It can't be!' Nicola murmured wonderingly.

She crossed the room and lifted the frame down from the wall.

Could these people possibly be Grandpa's relations? Yet how else could they have Gran's photo?

She carried it with her when she made her way back to the living-room once she'd dressed.

The old man was sitting at the table,

reading a newspaper. His wife was working on some crochet and keeping an eye on Carlo, squatting on a rug at her feet with a book of farm animals.

Nicola held out the photo to the man, wordlessly at first. He took it from her, and looked from her to the picture, then back again, his eyebrows raised quizzically.

'Those are my grandparents, my mother and my uncle,' Nicola said shakily, and the man exclaimed.

'Marta! Do you hear that? She's Marco's granddaughter!'

Shaken by the suddenly charged atmosphere, Carlo scrambled to his feet to cling to Nicola's skirt and she picked him up.

Marta, too, got up, exclaiming in wonder.

'Paolo, I told you she looks like our Rosina,' she declared, and turned to Nicola. 'Those are our daughter's clothes you're wearing, child. And so you belong to Marco — Paolo's brother?'

'Uncle Paul was named for you!' Nicola whispered to the man.

'Yes.' Tears flowed from Paulo's eyes, but he brushed away his wife's comforting hand and went out of the room.

His wife's eyes followed him sympathetically.

'Marco was his great hero, you know. But he went away from home when Paulo was only a little boy.'

It was all too much for Carlo, clasped in Nicola's arms. He gave vent to such a prolonged wail of sadness that, when Paulo returned, he found the two women torn between tears and laughter.

'Come now.' Paulo smiled at Nicola, calming them all down. 'You must tell us why you are here and everything that has happened.'

Nicola sat down, still holding Carlo close, took a deep breath, and began . . .

Marta brought coffee in the middle of the story. Telling it seemed to take a long time, for her great-uncle and aunt wanted to know all about Marco's family first, and kept exclaiming and offering opinions when it came to the kidnapping.

'The carabinieri have been here looking for you,' Paulo told her. 'They have been asking everywhere. But I said I hadn't seen you — you were so urgent that no-one should know you are here. Did I do right, *cara?*'

'Well, yes, thank you. But I think it may be all right now, because if they were looking for us, it could mean they have caught the kidnappers.'

'Can you be sure?' Paulo asked carefully. 'We should make sure. If you're fit enough to walk to the next village, I have a friend who will lend me his car. He has a phone, too. I can take you home. Do you want to set off now or should I phone the Ranieri villa first?'

Nicola hesitated.

'I don't know why, but I'm still afraid. I'm even imagining that those carabinieri you saw could have been impostors.'

She brushed her forehead with her free hand and shook her head.

'I'm scared to trust anyone now. Could we stay till it gets dark? Would you mind? And then could you drive us to the Ranieri villa? They'll be terribly worried about us.'

'I don't suppose two more hours will make any difference,' Paulo was beginning, when they were startled by a loud, urgent knocking at the kitchen door.

Nobody moved as they glanced anxiously at each other.

Marta's hand flew to her throat as a second knock resounded through the house.

This time Paolo leapt to his feet and signalled Nicola to take Carlo through to the bedroom. He went with them and saw them safe before he answered the door.

Apprehension coiled within Nicola as they crouched behind the bed. Her stomach tightened. All she could hear was the rumble of men's voices in the passageway. Carlo clung to her, and glancing at him, Nicola's heart went out to the little boy. His face was white and his eyes terrified.

She was soothing him when the door opened. Carlo peeped over her shoulder and then he let out a yell.

'Papa!'

He scrambled from her grasp and threw himself across the bed to hurl himself into his father's open arms.

Nicola stood up slowly, and found she had to sink down on the bed as her knees buckled beneath her.

Half dazed, she listened to the love-words Angelo was showering on his little son. The flesh seemed to have fallen away from Angelo's face, and there were new lines there, but his eyes were luminous with joy.

Finally he hitched Carlo on to one hip, and sat down beside her.

'Nicola! I can't believe you are both safe!' Tears choked his voice. 'I'm so thankful, so grateful to you . . . '

He ran out of words and held out his arms. Carlo at once copied him, and the three of them hugged each other.

Nicola felt strangely numb. She would have expected to feel relieved now, as Angelo clearly was, but she didn't really feel anything at all.

It was some time before she could pull away and allow father and son to have their own private reunion.

'Oh, Carlo, you're sure you're well? Nobody harmed you? Now I have you safe I'll never let you go again . . . '

'Papa! We were in a loft and Nicola set fire to it!'

Carlo was becoming wildly exuberant now that he was safely held against his father's chest, and Angelo smiled at him.

'I guessed that. What a wonderful guardian angel you have!'

'I love Nicola, Papa.' Carlo turned in his arms and held out a chubby hand to her.

'I can see that.' He smiled at her over Carlo's head. 'Nicola is very clever. She cares for you, and she helped us to catch some very bad men.'

'Did she, Papa?' Carlo butted his head into Angelo's shoulder, and his father's arms tightened around him.

'You deserve a medal, Nicola.' He smiled, but then his face changed, and his voice softened. 'I am very proud of you — and very thankful.'

Gazing at him, she suddenly wanted to smooth the lines of strain from his face and wipe away the tear-streaks as though he was Carlo. She had just enough self-control not to reach out to him; she knew it must only be a reaction to the peril she had been in.

Only now that Angelo was here, with Carlo safe, did she realise how very frightened she had been and for how long.

He began to ask her questions now in rapid-fire Italian, but in her current state of mental exhaustion her brain couldn't cope with the language. She had to answer in English, but they seemed to understand each other well enough.

There was a knock at the door, and Paolo came in.

'Marta is cooking. You would like a shower, Signor Ranieri?'

Angelo agreed at once, although he had difficulty unhooking the clinging Carlo from around his neck.

Eventually, though, the little boy consented to go to Nicola, and as she sat crooning to him until his father came back, she wondered how much damage these terrible days had done to the child.

She herself felt light-headed, as if she was seeing everything from a distance.

'I phoned the villa,' Angelo's voice said in her ear. 'Your mother is here. She and my father were out — in Amalfi, Raimondo thought — but I told him to say we will come right home.'

'Mum's here?' Nicola sagged with relief. 'How soon can we go back to the villa?'

186

Suddenly she was longing to hear her mother's voice.

But Marta couldn't do enough for Angelo. She wouldn't even let him phone for transport before she had fed him and produced coffee for them all.

They all sat around as Angelo ate, Nicola nursing Carlo, and Angelo told his side of the story.

'I wonder why you didn't find us after the fire?' Nicola was thinking how much strain she would have been spared if he had come sooner.

'When I heard the dog barking up in the woods, I thought perhaps I had found you. But then I saw the signore coming up to you, so I waited.'

'But why not come out into the open then?' Paolo asked, mystified.

'The trouble was, signore . . . Forgive me.' Angelo looked uncomfortable. 'You see, I didn't know who you were, or where you were taking them. You might have been one of the kidnappers' friends. Certainly I had no idea you would turn out to be the great-uncle of

Nicola!' They all laughed.

'So you were checking us out with your little telephone,' Paolo said, 'before you would come near the house?'

'I'm afraid so.'

'In the circumstances, I forgive you!' Paolo leaned forward. 'I am glad to have met you. And now I don't have to worry about getting the young ones home.'

'No, I'll phone for transport.' Angelo drained a second cup of Marta's strong coffee. 'There's a track from the village, isn't there?'

Paolo nodded.

'I am only sorry that Marco's granddaughter will be going home again so soon when we have only just met.' His brown eyes, filled with warmth and love, held Nicola's. 'Your mother will want to take you home, I think, *cara mia*?'

Nicola hadn't had time to think about what would happen next. She was still trying to get to grips with the fact that her mother was in the country, that she would see her soon.

Paolo looked at her white face, and sent Angelo the look of a stern patriarch.

'You cannot keep her here after what she has endured. She will recover more quickly in England, and . . . she will be safer there.'

Angelo nodded slowly, with apparent reluctance.

'Whatever Nicola wants . . . But first there will be some formalities with the police. My colleagues will want to talk to you, Nicola. You will help them?'

'Yes, of course.' She couldn't imagine talking about all this to anyone but Angelo, but then, she still felt so tired. Everything would be better if only she could see her mother . . .

★ ★ ★

Back in England, Gail couldn't free her mind of unease. She hadn't slept all night. Today was one of the days on which Steve still worked. He was silent and worried-looking at breakfast, and barely responded to her attempts at conversation.

She was relieved when the children came down in their pyjamas and started squabbling over the cereal.

'Who's looking after us today?' Emma asked between mouthfuls.

'I am,' Gail said sternly, 'and I won't be having any nonsense.'

'I didn't make any nonsense yesterday when I came home from school, did I, Daddy?' Christopher asked smugly.

'Not that I can remember.' Steve managed to grin at him. 'See and keep it up!'

The colleague who gave Steve a lift to work hooted at the door, and once they had left Gail began to get the children ready for their day.

Emma twitched as the hastily-applied brush caught in the tangles of her hair.

'When we've taken Chris to school, can we go to the play park, Mummy?'

Wearily Gail laid the brush down.

'Maybe. Hurry up, Christopher! David and John will be waiting! Have you got all your things together now?'

There was an ominous silence.

Gail sighed, and started to look for him.

As she feared he had gone to ground under his bed.

She spent ages trying to coax him to come out, with a mixture of threats and bribes. It was only when, in exasperation, she walked away and ignored him that Christopher decided that his school pals might miss him if he wasn't there.

The boys yelled at each other all the way to school in the car and Gail's head began to pound. It was only by a supreme effort of will that she forced herself not to yell at them to be quiet.

With the boys safely inside the school gate, she drove off to the supermarket where her nagging worry about what could have taken her mother to Italy was temporarily swallowed up in the smaller one of shopping to feed her family well on their reduced budget.

It was the logistics of it all that was beginning to get to her: juggling Emma's delicate health, Christopher's mini-rebellions, Steve's fears for the future . . .

Running things at home along with her part-time job — she should be able to take that in her stride — but . . .

'What is it, Emma?' The girl was tugging at her sleeve.

'When are we going to the swing park, Mummy?' she pleaded.

'I don't know, lovely.' Gail took a hand off the wheel to rub her damp forehead. 'Maybe when we're finished the shopping — we'll see.'

'Granny Gwen would take me,' Emma grumbled, and Gail's face cleared.

Gran! Of course! Why hadn't she thought of that herself? She could talk to her grandmother.

'How would you like to go to visit Granny Gwen once we've done the shopping and tidied up the house?' she asked.

Emma gave this some thought. She was totally Christopher's opposite — his reaction would have been instant.

'OK!' she finally agreed. Granny Gwen kept special toys in a drawer for her, and never minded when she got covered with chocolate.

★ ★ ★

'Darlings!' Gwen, still in her housecoat, having spent the night on guard at The Rose, hugged Gail and stooped to pick up Emma, who responded angelically.

Ushering them in, she insisted on getting orange juice and biscuits for Emma and opening the toy drawer for her. Then she fetched coffee for herself and Gail.

'This is a lovely surprise!' she said as she sat down. 'I can't think when you last popped in to visit me like this. And don't worry about your mother, dear — I did some sleuthing last night!'

193

'Don't worry?' Gail lifted anguished eyes. 'Gran, I just don't seem to be able to stop worrying. Everything's going wrong, and I so need to talk to Mum.'

'Talk to me, darling. Oh, thank you, pet.' Gwen smiled at Emma, who was systematically emptying the drawer and carrying all the toys over to her.

Holding a dog-eared teddy, Gwen gazed at Gail's face. She did look harassed, poor thing. Yet someone as young as she was should still be carefree and going on Greek holidays with her friends and having holiday romances . . .

'You'd better tell me everything,' Gwen said firmly. 'But your mum's all right. She's gone to see Nicola — Karen Mason told me so last night.'

'Then Mr Mason deliberately misled me!' Gail burst out. 'I'm sure he said Mum had gone on business. Though, mind you — ' she thought back ' — he did say personal business. But why's she suddenly dashed off to see Nicky?'

Gwen shrugged. 'Perhaps she's ill. I

just know your mum told Mr Mason that she didn't want to worry either of us. If she had wanted us to phone, she would have let us know exactly what she was doing and why.'

'But if Nicola were ill Mum wouldn't have kept us in the dark about it.' Gail looked suddenly afraid. 'It's got to be something else — something worse.'

'Now calm down, darling.' Gwen took a battered Ludo box from Emma. 'We'll hear something soon. Richard Mason is flying out to be with her — he's probably on his way by now. Try not to worry.'

'Try not to worry!' Gail fumed to herself, as she left to pick the boys up for lunch. 'Well, no matter what Gran says, I'm not waiting any longer. I'm going to phone the Ranieris tonight.'

★   ★   ★

Nicola knew she ought to be deliriously happy, but she just wanted to burst into tears. She had never been so relieved in

195

all her life as when the police car drove up to the villa and she was able to run into her mother's arms.

Mothers were funny, though. Linda's first words were, 'Oh, darling! Your hair!'

Well, of course it was awful. It was grubby and tangled. But that wasn't quite what Nicola had expected after all she and Carlo had been through.

Soon they were inside the villa and her mother's comforting arms were still around her. Vaguely she heard the babble of Italian surrounding Carlo, with Giorgio's deep tones booming above it, and then Carlo's tired wail, receding as he was carried up to bed.

Angelo came into the room.

'They're coming back to talk to you tomorrow, Nicola. OK?'

She was too tired even to answer him. He came over, knelt down and looked into her eyes, reading there what the others couldn't.

'She must go and rest now,' he said firmly to Linda. 'It can take time to recover from what she has been through.'

He took Nicola's hands. 'On your feet, Nicola. Come — we'll go upstairs. You'll be better once you rest.'

Leaving Linda surprised and a little miffed, he guided Nicola to her room and sat down beside her.

'I know how you're feeling, Nicola,' he told her gently. 'You're still in shock, you know. You feel strange, shy, vulnerable, yet along with the relief, you still feel afraid.'

Nicola stared at him, wide-eyed.

'That's exactly it! How do you understand so well?' She felt the tears starting to her eyes again. 'I can't even face eating with everyone tonight . . .'

'Of course you can't. There is no question of that. Papa has called the doctor, anyway. Stay here as long as you need to. Have as many baths as you like.'

'Oh!' She drew a ragged breath. 'I can wash my hair at last!'

'As often as you want.'

'Angelo, I'm scared! Why do I suddenly want to cut it all off?'

'Your hair?' He caught a dark, curling strand and smiled at her. 'That would be a pity,' he murmured. 'It's a reaction to the stress, of course. That's why you feel like this. Getting free is never the end of a kidnapping.'

'What I can't get rid of is the guilt. I thought I was taking every precaution. I never took my eyes off Carlo for a moment after you warned me. I'll never get over the feeling that I failed you!' The last words came out in a wail.

'Nicola!' His words were sharp and he took her hands in his. 'You couldn't have stopped them. When kidnappers are determined to take somebody, they will take them. You did more than my father and I could ever have asked, *cara*.' His voice dropped. 'You kept Carlo safe — and yourself — and you got away from them. And the fire — all your doing — if it hadn't been for the fire we would never have caught up with those men.

'So you see, you did right, not wrong. Thanks to you, my son is safe and well.'

Tears trembled on her cheeks, and Angelo drew her towards him for a brief hug.

'Have your bath, *cara*. By the time your hair is dry the doctor will be here.'

And he was, a nice, kindly, older man who examined her briskly, asked questions sympathetically and listened to her answers.

'I feel very odd — as if I were made of thin crystal and might shatter at any moment. I tried so hard to look after Carlo, you know . . . ' Tears filled her eyes. 'I couldn't believe it was happening . . . ' She covered her face with her hands. 'And there was no bathroom . . . '

'I understand,' he said softly. 'That is by design, to undermine your self-respect.'

He was kind and he had the healing touch. How else could she have confided in him like this?

He said the same things that Angelo

had said, that she was still suffering from shock and mustn't expect too much of herself.

He produced ointment for the cuts and bruises, and left sleeping pills in case she needed them.

'Physically she is fine,' he told Linda as he was about to leave. 'Otherwise, time is the great healer. Don't be impatient with any irrational behaviour in either her or little Carlo. Thank God their ordeal didn't last longer.'

The doctor's words relieved Linda in a way, but she was still worried when she went to recount his words to Giorgio. With the understanding that had built up between them over the endless hours of waiting, he knew how she was feeling, and sympathetically put his arm round her.

'You must stay here as long as it takes to get Nicola well again — even if it's all summer. Please, Linda. It would please me very much. I would love you to stay.'

She gazed at him.

'I don't know, Giorgio. Nicky might want to go home. And I do have another life at home ... my other daughter, my work ...'

As she spoke, she felt that it was indeed another life — Gail and Steve's worries, Gwen and the fight for The Rose ...

Giorgio put his arms round her.

'I want to get to know you, Linda. Stay for a little holiday, please.'

He drew her gently into his embrace, but just as Linda was about to rest her head against his shoulder, she caught sight of Richard Mason framed in the doorway.

★ ★ ★

That evening, once the children were in bed, Gail looked out the phone number of the Villa Ranieri. She would never have a better opportunity to phone. She needed to hear her mother's voice — not knowing what was going on was driving her crazy.

Gail had never taken as much interest as the others in Italian, and was thrown by the Ranieri butler's rapid recitation of, '*Villa Ranieri. Pronto! Chi parla?*' all run together.

She took a second to sort out the key word, Ranieri, and then said very carefully who she was, and asked if she might speak with Mrs Linda Gray.

'She is engaged at the moment, but I will see if she can come to speak to you.'

Her mother's voice, coming over the phone, sounded breathless and agitated.

'Gail! How did you know I was here? What's the matter?'

'What do you mean, 'What's the matter?'' Gail snapped. 'Why didn't you tell us you were going to Italy? Has something happened to Nicky — is she all right?'

'It's all right, love. They're home and she's fine. I didn't want any of you worrying . . . How did you know?'

'Gran got some garbled story Karen

202

had teased out of her father. You said 'they' were home — who's 'they' and where had they been?'

Linda drew in her breath shakily.

'Oh, Gail, it's a very long story. Nicola and little Carlo were kidnapped — but they're both safe. Nicky managed to escape.'

Gail didn't know whether she was on her head or her heels. Explanations and exclamations filled the next few minutes.

'I can't believe Nicky found help from Grandpa's brother! And you're sure I can't talk to her? She is all right, Mum, isn't she? There's nothing you're not telling me?'

'She's fine, I promise. She's just tired. She was fast asleep when I looked in and that's the best thing for her.'

'When will you be home?' Gail was longing to see her mother face to face.

Linda hesitated before admitting, 'I don't know, dear. Giorgio — Signor Ranieri, Carlo's grandfather — wants me to stay for a while. Now that

Richard is here, I can ask him about that.'

'Mr Mason's with you?'

'He arrived today. He came out to try to help me. It was very kind of him. He arrived just after Nicola and Carlo had got home and the place was in an uproar.

'Look, dear, I'll have to go. It's nearly time for dinner. I've left the two men having drinks and I think I'd better get back.'

'Mum, are you all right? You sound a bit . . . hectic.'

'I'm fine, dear, really. I suppose I'm just so relieved that Nicola's all right that I'm a bit euphoric! Darling, will you let your gran know everything, please? Tell her I'll call her as soon as I can.'

'I'll do that. Love to Nicky.'

'Bye! Love to Steve and the children!'

Gail hung up, still bewildered but as elated as her mother.

Thank goodness everything was OK! Maybe her mum had been right not to want to worry them ... She tried to imagine what her state of mind would have been if she had known that Nicola, her little sister, was in danger, and shivered.

She lost no time in ringing her grandmother.

Gwen answered with her usual happy telephone voice but her tone changed when she heard Gail speak.

'Oh, it's you.'

'Sorry to disappoint you! Who were you expecting?'

'Oh, Gail,' Gwen mourned, 'they've all deserted me! Most of the campaign team have gone off on a Historic Cities tour. I ask you! Just when the balloon's about to go up!'

'Well, why didn't you go, too? You'd have enjoyed it, wouldn't you?'

'Because I'm loyal and faithful to our own town. Somebody has to stay here and see justice done ... Besides, I thought Rod would be helping me, but he's gone down with a recurrence of his malaria — at just the wrong moment.'

She paused for a moment. 'Look, Gail, the reason I'm so upset is that I've heard the bulldozers are on the point of moving in, and the preservation order isn't here yet.'

'Gran, I'm sorry about all this, but it's not why I'm calling,' Gail said patiently. 'I've spoken to Mum. You're never going to believe this . . . '

★ ★ ★

When Gwen hung up, she wasn't sure she did believe it. She felt quite shaken.

'Marco's brother,' she whispered. 'Little Paolo. Oh, Marco!'

She crossed the room to pick up the photograph of the family — the very one Nicky had found in Paolo and Marta's bedroom.

'Marco,' she said softly, caressingly. 'How you would have rejoiced at this moment. I must see Paolo . . . for your sake.'

She had to sit down for a minute, and then she went to make a cup of tea.

The photograph was close by her hand all the time, and she placed it beside the tray when she sat down in the living-room.

As she sipped her tea, her eyes were on the handsome husband she had so adored and loved to lean on.

In the photo he was at the height of his strength. Suddenly she missed him more acutely than she had done for ages.

She sat there through her second cup of tea, thinking. Then she lifted the photo again.

'*Caro mio*,' she whispered. 'I have so much to remember — so much to thank you for.'

Her panic about The Rose had disappeared. She saw quite clearly what her life had become.

Her family would always be important to her, and yes, they needed her, they always would. But she had begun the fight for The Rose for herself. And that had brought Rodney into her life.

She smiled again, this time with a

hint of mischief.

'Chalk and cheese, Marco, that's what you and Rodney are. And Rod doesn't know me yet as you did. But he will!'

Feeling much better, she went for her coat, keys and bag. Rodney's malaria was not going to get in the way of anything Gwen Moretti had set her heart on — the fight for The Rose, or anything else!

'Tired Of Being Alone . . . '

Linda Gray had never spent a more uncomfortable half-hour in her life. Why could life never be simple and straightforward? Why couldn't she be left alone to enjoy her heartfelt joy at having Nicola returned to her?

When she had seen Richard standing in the doorway, her heart had stood still. It was unfortunate that Giorgio's arms had been encircling her just then, but surely Richard understood how different the Italians were from English men? Touching meant the same as a word or a look at home.

When Linda returned from her phone conversation with Gail, Giorgio was just finishing bringing Richard more or less up to date with what had happened.

'You have all my sympathy,' Richard was saying as she came in. 'I'm a father myself and if that had been Karen — '

When, in turn, Giorgio was called to the phone, Linda tried to thank Richard.

'You'll never know how grateful I am.' She looked into his steady blue eyes earnestly. 'You've been so thoughtful, coming out like this. And trying to reassure Gail as well . . . '

'I don't think you needed me,' he said quietly, and Linda felt a pang of regret.

I did, in a way, she thought. But how can I begin to explain?

It was almost a relief when Giorgio came back.

'Angelo can't join us for dinner. I'm sorry, Linda. He — '

Richard rose. 'I'm sorry but I can't stay either, signore. Thank you so much for the drinks. Now that I know that everything is all right, I must return to my host in Naples.'

Linda was dismayed to find that she was actually relieved that Richard wasn't staying for dinner.

'Then why don't you come and have lunch with Linda and Nicola here tomorrow instead?' Giorgio asked cordially. 'I must get back to business now this is over, and I'm sure you have much to discuss.'

Richard accepted the invitation equally graciously, and Linda watched him walk along the terrace, suddenly aware of an unexplained ache in her heart.

★ ★ ★

That lunch on the terrace of the Ranieri villa should have been a pleasant meal but Linda, conscious all the time of the extreme politeness between Giorgio and Richard Mason, and still worried about Nicola, who was pale and silent, couldn't enjoy any of it.

They had just finished eating when she was summoned to take a phone call from England, and after that everything else flew out of her mind.

'Nicky!' she announced as she

hurried back out to the terrace. 'We have to go home at once. Gran's been arrested!'

'Arrested?' Richard exclaimed.

'But why?' Nicola stared at her. Her own ordeal was so recent that her mother's words had set her nerves jangling.

'Something to do with her campaign.' Linda's voice shook. 'Gail didn't tell me exactly. Anyway, I have to get home at once.'

'We'll get the first available flights,' Richard assured her, 'even if we have to fly from Rome or Pisa. I'll see to it . . . '

He reached out a comforting hand to hers, and Linda looked at him gratefully. It was wonderful having him there at that moment.

She had difficulty in dragging her attention back to her daughter.

'We'll have to pack, Nicky — '

'No!' Carlo screamed, making them all jump. 'Nicola not go!' He scrambled down from his chair and threw his arms round her waist. 'Don't go, Nicola!

Don't go!' he squealed, becoming almost hysterical.

'It's all right, Carlo!' She stroked his head tenderly. 'I'm not going anywhere.'

She gathered him into her arms and tried to still his trembling, but he was distraught.

I can't leave him, she thought, tears choking her. I can't leave him!

'Papa! Papa!' Carlo stretched out his arms to Angelo, who had just come out of the house. 'Nicola not to go!'

Angelo took his son from her and cuddled him.

'Ssh, Carlo. Why make such a fuss? How can Nicola leave when a nice policeman is coming to talk to her?'

Linda sat down. Her eyes met her daughter's, and she felt totally helpless.

'I just want to take you home safely along with me, Nicky,' she said softly. 'You can understand that, can't you, Signor Ranieri?'

Angelo was frowning.

'You are going home now?' He shot a

glance at Giorgio. 'I thought you would stay for a little while?'

Giorgio excused himself politely and went into the house, while Linda told Angelo what had happened.

'Please don't think we're a parcel of rogues.' Linda's smile was charming, even in these circumstances, Richard thought. 'I think my mother must have become over-zealous in pursuit of her campaign — annoyed the police, probably.'

Cradling Carlo, who was quieter now, sucking his thumb as he rested against his shoulder, Angelo smiled back at her.

'Papa will be disappointed. He was planning a trip to Capri for you, I know.'

Faint colour swept into Linda's cheeks and she didn't look at Richard.

'I must go, Angelo. I'm very sorry to leave in such haste, but I must find out what's happening.'

'We have a contact in a travel agency. I'll get in touch right now. Two seats or three? You want Nicola to go with you . . . today?'

'Yes,' said Linda, just as Nicola said, 'No.'

Carlo gave a long, gulping sigh and settled his head more comfortably on his father's shoulder. He blinked twice, then his eyes remained closed, damp lashes fanning out across his cheeks.

Linda looked at her daughter's face as she gazed at Carlo.

No, she won't leave him, she thought, and how could I expect her to, after what they've been through together?

There were so many feelings bubbling up, pulling her in every direction.

Richard, on the other hand, looked wonderfully controlled, calmly drinking coffee while watching the antics of a lizard on the hot tiles. He needed her, too. She remembered that contract he was after . . . she ought to be back at work helping him to win it.

Her mother needed her, Gail did, too, but Nicola . . .

She wanted, most of all, to have

Nicky safe at home, and hear her infectious laugh again. She would even be happy to see her whizzing off on Fraser Blyth's motor-bike.

'I'll just get Anna.' Angelo rose with Carlo. 'It's his siesta time.' He smiled over the little boy's head at Richard. 'Come with me, Richard, and we'll see what can be arranged.'

As the men went into the house, Nicola rose and gave her mother a hug.

'I must just talk to Angelo before this policeman arrives to question me.'

Linda's arms tightened round her.

'I know, darling, it's all right. I was being selfish. You must stay, for Carlo.'

Nicola bestowed one of her rare kisses on her mother's hair.

'Thanks, Mum.'

★ ★ ★

She ran into the villa and caught up with Angelo.

'Angelo — when they talk to me, will you be there?' She wanted to add,

216

'Please don't leave me!'

'I'll be here,' he reassured her, as though he had heard her unspoken plea.

Nicola sat for a while with Carlo. Linda looked in briefly to say that Angelo had found them a flight for late that night and she was just going for a siesta to prepare for it. The next time the door opened, it was Angelo, to tell her the officers had arrived.

'You'll like Signor Todini,' he said as he accompanied her downstairs. 'He's a very good policeman.'

Sensing her desire to bolt, he stopped and took her arm. She gazed at him with mute appeal.

'They're waiting,' he said gently. 'Any detail, anything you may have overheard — whatever you can think of might help them to make more arrests.'

She looked like a figure from a dream, he thought, as she moved. The turquoise haze of her Indian-cotton dress floated around her . . . her cheeks too pale, her eyes too large . . .

'I'm scared,' she whispered.

'There's no need to be. You are the strong one, Nicola. You're the one who beat your captors — the only person I know who would have got out of that alive!'

Bolstered by his praise, she straightened her shoulders as he opened the door for her.

There were two officers, an older man and a woman about Nicola's age.

To begin with she sat, amazed, as they praised her fulsomely and thanked her for her 'brilliant' actions which had led them to making their arrests.

Todini was a middle-aged family man, but he had a generous dash of Italian charm and did his best to put her at her ease.

'Could you go back to when you were on the beach with Carlo that day, signorina, and tell us everything from there . . . ?'

She shivered and nodded.

It was a long process. When she couldn't find the Italian word, she used an English one, and Angelo translated. She spoke slowly as she searched for accuracy, and the woman had no difficulty in taking notes.

As Nicola struggled to remember — words, names, church bells, a dog barking, a cockerel crowing — her eyes kept seeking Angelo's. She was thankful for his presence, his smiling encouragement gave her strength.

At last the officers seemed satisfied and thanked her profusely as they rose.

'My card.' Todini handed it to her. 'If you remember anything else, call me. I'll come back any time.'

While Angelo saw them out, Nicola stayed where she was, too drained to move. He found her there when he returned.

'Tired?' There was sympathy in his eyes.

'Shattered!'

'Would you like some brandy?'

'Angelo, I'd like to go to the hairdresser in Sorrento. And I'd like to drown in a gallon of perfume. I feel like

I'll never smell sweet again!'

'Nonsense!' he told her robustly. 'Rest now. Tomorrow — the hairdresser. As for smelling sweet, you do, but I'll bring you some perfume if that's what you want. Shall I bring the brandy, too?'

His head was tilted, teasing her.

She summoned up a smile.

'I think I will have some, please.'

★ ★ ★

When Linda was finally packed and ready to leave, she went along to Nicola's room.

'Nicky?'

There was no answer but she followed a slight noise to the bathroom.

Nicola was standing at the mirror.

'Won't you change your mind and come with us?' Linda was saying as she came in but then she stopped and gasped.

'I can't leave,' Nicola said distantly. She had scissors in her hand, and Linda couldn't look away from her head. She had hacked off her beautiful hair — the strands lay in the basin in front of her — and was left with a ragged urchin crop.

'I couldn't wait for tomorrow,' was all she said.

In spite of the late-night flight, Giorgio insisted on driving Linda and Richard to Naples airport.

All evening, Giorgio had been sending her long, reproachful looks, which she had been avoiding.

If Nicky and Carlo had been out of touch for much longer — or if, heaven forbid, they hadn't come back — Linda knew she might easily have succumbed to the solace of Giorgio's arms. But it would have been a terrible mistake — for both of them. She knew that, too.

At the airport, she let him kiss her. Richard, a discreet distance away, didn't hear his soft farewell.

'Come back, soon, *cara*. Please.'

During the flight, she closed her eyes,

only to have glittering images tantalise her.

One moment it was the sun piercing through the patio vines, tracing leaf patterns of sunlight and shade on her legs and arms.

Next she was in the cathedral again, her heart reaching out to the kneeling figure beside her.

Then the sea was before her, pink at dawn, then emerald, wine-dark at midnight . . .

She'd gathered Nicola close before they left, trying to hide her distress, touching the shorn head with a whimsical smile.

'Don't worry,' Angelo had murmured to her as she had said her farewells. 'Nicola and Carlo will not go out alone now.'

Torn between looking back longingly and anxiety to have the journey over, she suddenly became acutely aware of Richard's presence, disturbingly near, in the seat on her right.

She tried to sleep, but in a little while

she heard him speaking, so softly that she couldn't catch what he said.

'Sorry?'

'I said I'm an expert at mismanaging my emotional life.'

She sat up and stared at him. Never, even after their evening out, had he spoken to her like this before.

But just then the hostess reached them with food. After all she had been through, the last thing Linda wanted to do was eat, but the coffee was welcome.

'Now, Giorgio Ranieri,' Richard said, lifting his coffee cup slowly to his lips. 'I can't imagine him getting *his* emotions in a muddle . . . '

'He was very worried and very vulnerable when I went out . . . '

His eyes searched hers.

'And you consoled him?'

'He tried to console me. We tried to console each other,' she said firmly, insistently. 'We might never have seen Nicola or Carlo again!'

'I'm sorry, Linda,' he said gently, looking remorseful. 'I wasn't thinking.

Forgive me. You must have felt so alone.'

'Oh, yes.' She tried to will the tears away from her eyes. 'That's it exactly. It's a long time since Alan died, and I'm so tired of making decisions alone . . . '

He took her hand and held it firmly, comfortingly.

'I'll never be able to thank you properly for coming out to help me, Richard,' she told him sincerely. 'And you risked losing an important contract to do it! I feel very humble.'

She didn't look at him as she spoke. She was afraid that if she did, her hand would reach up and smooth the furrows from his brow . . .

Policemen At The Door

'I honestly don't know how I got up there, Linda. It must have been a rush of adrenaline.' Gwen Moretti's eyes were bright and she was chattering non-stop. 'One minute I was on top of the porch and then I must have clambered up on to the roof!'

'Oh, Mum!' Linda looked at her in despair. 'I thought I was going to have to stand bail for you and guarantee your good behaviour! Gail said . . . '

'I know! They wanted to know my next of kin. I told them Gail, but afterwards I thought of Rodney, and he sent his lawyer. So he took care of everything, and I haven't been charged.'

'What on earth were you doing, Mum?' Linda asked weakly.

Gwen opened her eyes wide.

'I wanted to attract people's attention, of course! I knew when the

225

bulldozers arrived that I had to use delaying tactics till the preservation order reached the council offices.' Her eyes twinkled. 'Oh, they were upset! The things they yelled at me!'

Linda shook her head.

'I yelled back at them that the preservation order was on its way,' Gwen rattled on.

'And when did they call the police?'

'Well, it was getting light, and they had to do the work before the High Street got busy. One of them got on his mobile phone . . . ' Gwen frowned. 'It was all a bit confusing after that. D'you think I'm getting old?'

Linda gazed at her determined, energetic and definitely indomitable mother.

'Certainly not! Anyone would have got confused at that point.'

'Well, the police asked me — quite nicely, I must say — to come down, but when I couldn't — my legs wouldn't move by then — they sent for the fire brigade.

'By the time they got there and climbed up to get me, the shops were opening, the street was getting busy and everybody was crowding round to see what was going on.'

'Oh, Mum! How embarrassing!'

'Not at all!' Gwen protested. 'It was good. I shouted down what it was all about, and they all took my side and started chanting 'Leave the old inn alone!'' Her eyes sparkled at the memory. 'It was the most marvellous thing! Mind you, I didn't like it so much when they called, 'Leave the old lady alone!' I don't think I look old!'

'You don't! It was just their way of getting sympathy, I'm sure,' Linda soothed.

'And I didn't mean to knock that policeman's spectacles off. That was an accident.'

'I expect it was,' Linda agreed wryly.

'But then they — er — took me in.' Gwen shook her head. 'It was so disconcerting. I never expected to hear that caution — you know, the one you hear on TV — being said to me!'

Linda was torn between laughter and tears, and Gwen noticed.

'Don't worry, dear. It was all for the best. The preservation order duly arrived, as I knew it would, and the council are bound to be feeling like fools. There was no need for confrontation at all.'

Linda began to laugh helplessly and Gwen looked at her in concern.

'Now, now, dear. Don't get hysterical. I'll get you some more coffee, shall I — you look shattered!'

'I am a bit,' Linda conceded and followed her mother into the kitchen. 'But I want to go in to work after lunch. I'll have a bit of a backlog to clear up, I expect.'

As Gwen filled the kettle, the doorbell rang. Linda went to answer it, and led Rodney Bingham through to the kitchen.

'All right, Gwen?' he asked.

She turned to smile at him.

'Thank you so much for sending your

lawyer, Rodney. Oh, you still look awfully pale! Are you sure you should be out of bed?'

'I'm fine. I came round because I've had an idea about The Rose . . . '

He turned courteously to Linda. 'Everything's all right now in Italy?'

'Absolutely,' she said cheerfully, fingers crossed behind her back. 'So what's this idea about The Rose?'

They took their coffee cups through to the sitting-room and settled down.

'Local radio is saying the council may make the old inn into a museum. Well, I know a few small towns that have museums like that.' He looked at Gwen. 'I thought it would be fun for you and me to go off for a holiday and see how these things are done. A week or two perhaps?'

'What a great idea!' exclaimed Linda, relief at the thought of Rodney taking charge of her mother flooding through her. 'Don't you think so, Mum?'

'That would be very nice, Rodney,' Gwen agreed and Linda looked at her sharply. She knew that tone of voice. What was her mother plotting now?

★ ★ ★

Although, sure enough, a small mountain of work awaited Linda, she found solace in being back at her desk. For the time being she could shut out everything else and concentrate on the mail that had accumulated in her absence.

By three o'clock she had a sizeable pile of items that needed Richard's attention and she hoped he would soon be back from lunch.

He still hadn't appeared when Karen bounced in.

'Dad here?'

'He's not back from lunch yet. A business lunch. Would you like to wait? He shouldn't be long.'

Karen flopped onto a chair and stretched out her long legs.

'I really like your mother, Mrs Gray,' she announced. 'Your daughters are lucky. She's my idea of a Supergran!'

'Life's never dull when Mum's around.' Linda smiled briefly. 'But this time she's really got me worried.'

'Don't be. She was great! I've written the most marvellous article. Fraser Blyth phoned me that morning. He'd set off to help her, and got a puncture. He was scared to abandon his bike in case it got stolen, and he called me to go along instead.'

Linda put down her pen and concentrated on Karen.

'I arrived just as the police got there. The crowd didn't need much encouragement to start chanting.'

Linda closed her eyes. What had made her think that work would offer an escape from her problems?

'I got some marvellous shots with Dad's camera. 'Brave Champion Defends Historic Inn . . . ' D'you like that?'

'You're not going to print a picture of Mum on the roof, are you?' Linda asked faintly.

'Of course! It's my first big chance to

impress the editor. I bet it makes the front page!'

'What does?' Richard asked, coming in.

'Dad, I've got a brilliant exclusive — Linda's mother on the roof of the inn! Being in the know, of course, I have all the background.' She jumped up, brimming over with enthusiasm. 'They'll probably offer me a permanent job. I'm the luckiest person alive to get a break like this!'

Richard saw the anguish in Linda's eyes and turned to his daughter.

'I don't think Linda wants that article to run, Karen,' he warned, and saw her face flush.

'But you can't spoil my big break!' she protested in disbelief.

'Of course not!' Linda agreed hastily. 'I wouldn't spoil things for you. I just wish my mother didn't go to such extremes.'

She managed a shaky smile, and Richard touched her shoulder.

'Come round and have dinner with

us tonight, Linda. We need to talk.'

'That's very kind of you, but I have to be at Gail's.' She sighed with some regret. 'I promised.'

'Well, later. For coffee?' he suggested.

'Yes, well, I could pop in on my way home.'

'I'm going out. To a disco,' Karen announced.

'Well, I might catch you before you go,' Linda suggested with a smile as they disappeared into Richard's office.

* * *

Gail threw herself into her mother's arms the minute she set foot over the threshold.

'Oh, Mum! I'm so glad you're back! Emma's coughing, Steve's terribly depressed and Christopher is being impossible. I'm nearly out of my mind!'

Linda patted her back and drew away to look at her.

'If it's that bad, I don't know what help I can be.'

'Your just being here helps. Wait and see — Steve will be bright, Christopher will behave like an angel and Emma won't cough once!'

She led the way to the kitchen.

'Come and keep me company while I finish getting the supper. They're all in the garden . . . Tell me about Nicola, and Italy, and the Moretti relations. Tell me about Gran!'

Linda laughed. 'Where shall I start?'

Gail's prophecy about her family's behaviour turned out to be uncannily accurate. Emma didn't cough once during the meal, Christopher ate his food like a gentleman, and Steve even managed a hopeful smile when Linda asked how things were going.

'We've had a few redundancies, but so far they've been voluntary, thank goodness, and now we're all waiting to hear if this new order will be confirmed.'

Gail looked up.

'You didn't tell me there was hope of a new order.'

'I couldn't.' He met her eyes. 'It seemed unlucky. It's a dreadful feeling wondering if it will come to us or not. We're afraid that if we breathe on it, it'll go away . . . Let's talk about something else. What's this about Granny Gwen, Linda?'

'Wait till you hear the details,' Gail said with relish. 'I'll bet it'll be all over the local paper.'

Linda's account of Gwen's exploits turned out to be excellent medicine for Steve, bringing a rare smile to his face.

The children listened, wide-eyed, and Gail caught Christopher's eye.

'Don't even think about it, Christopher,' she said sternly. 'Granny Gwen's old enough to decide to do something stupid. You are going nowhere near the roof!'

The family was still in a state of happy good humour when Linda left to go on to the Masons'.

As she drove to their grey stone villa, she realised she was much too tired to be going visiting. She'd had next to no sleep last night. Why on earth had she said she would go?

As Richard let her in, Karen appeared in the hall, ready for the disco.

'I'll get your coffee before I go,' she offered and went off to the kitchen while Richard guided Linda into the comfortable lounge.

'Would you rather have a drink?' he asked.

'Not unless you want me to collapse in a heap on the carpet. I'm asleep on my feet! Aren't you?'

'To tell you the truth, I am.'

He smiled as he went to put some music on and they both sat silently enjoying the relaxing melody until Karen came in with a tray.

Linda sat up when she saw the young man behind Karen.

'Fraser! Hello! Are you off to the disco, too?'

His eyes lit up at the sight of her.

'I said I'd give Karen a lift down,

yes.' He sat down beside her. 'But there was an ulterior motive. I wanted to ask how Nicky is. I haven't heard from her . . . though Mrs Moretti's kept me up to date. She is OK, isn't she?' he asked with real concern.

'Well, yes — at least, she will be. She's not quite over it all yet, you know, Fraser. What she went through was hair-raising, and both she and the little boy suffered — psychologically as much as physically. You'll have to give her a bit of time to recover.'

'I would've thought she'd want to come home to recover,' he muttered.

'She didn't want to leave Carlo — the little boy,' Linda said gently. 'He was in such a state at the thought of losing her. I'm sure she'll write — it's just a bit soon.'

He gazed at her as if weighing up her words.

'I just have a feeling, Mrs Gray. I didn't want her to go in the first place — and now I feel she may never be coming back.'

Linda laughed. 'Oh, Fraser, what nonsense!'

But all the same, his words left her with an uneasy feeling.

She tried to banish it after he and Karen had left. Her eyes kept closing until finally she turned to Richard.

'D'you mind if I shut my eyes for five minutes, Richard? If I don't, I'll be a lethal driver on the way home.'

'D'you mind if I join you over there and close mine, too? The music is so soothing, isn't it?'

He moved to sit beside her on the settee as she eased into the soft cushions and drifted away . . .

★ ★ ★

They woke simultaneously hours later.

'Two o'clock! Oh, my goodness, Richard — I must go!'

'Hush,' he said, stretching his arms luxuriously. 'Don't go yet. Maybe it's time to talk.'

'Not just now. I must get home.'

She tried to get to her feet, but he caught her arm and pulled her down again.

'Perhaps you're right. We don't need to talk, do we?'

Then he was gathering her firmly into his arms, and she melted against him.

'Let me kiss you, Linda,' he murmured. 'You're as aware as I am of what's here, what there could be between us. Don't let's pretend any longer that nothing exists.'

Then he was kissing her, and she didn't want him ever to stop . . .

She had no idea how long they'd been sitting there together when there was a loud knock on the door.

'Oh, Lord!' Richard groaned. 'I suppose Karen's forgotten her key again . . .'

Linda straightened the cushions, smoothed her hair and took a few deep breaths. Her head was spinning. She had never expected this.

She expected Karen to pop her head

round the door at any minute but although she waited, no-one came. She heard the rumble of men's voices in the hall, and when eventually the door did open, Richard came into the room followed by two policemen. They seemed to fill the room.

Glancing at Richard, she gasped — he seemed to have aged ten years in as many minutes.

'There's been an accident,' he said heavily. 'Karen and Fraser are both in hospital.'

Linda was on her feet at once.

'I'll come with you to the hospital. I mean, I'll follow in my car. Are they in the General?'

Richard just nodded.

★   ★   ★

Linda followed the police car taking him over to Fieldbridge General.

An accident and emergency unit in the middle of the night. Nurses in quiet shoes. A strange hive of activity in artificial daylight. Rows of chairs seating anxious relatives . . . What a frail thing the human body is, Linda thought in despair.

The woman at the desk told her Richard was already with Karen, and she looked around.

She thought the middle-aged couple at the end of a row might be Fraser's parents. The man looked a bit like Fraser . . .

He caught her eye, and she approached hesitantly.

'Excuse me — are you Fraser's parents?'

He nodded, and his wife gazed up at her, the strain showing in her eyes.

'I'm Nicola's mother,' Linda told them quietly, and sat down beside Mrs Blyth.

'We're waiting to hear about him.' Mrs Blyth managed a watery smile. 'You must be glad it wasn't Nicola on Fraser's bike. She's safely in Italy, isn't she?'

The irony of that stunned Linda, but

she controlled herself and murmured something non-committal.

'I'm always telling him to be careful,' Mr Blyth said angrily.

'I'm sorry about the accident,' Linda said gently, 'but it may not have been Fraser's fault. He's such an experienced biker.'

'I just hope it wasn't,' his father said helplessly. 'We don't know how that young girl is yet . . . '

Mrs Blyth rose and drifted to the window with Linda in her wake.

They stood there staring down into the darkness.

'Graham's still terribly disappointed with Fraser for dropping out of college,' Mrs Blyth said in an undertone. 'He's a very clever boy, but I think he went in the wrong direction. It should have been art or something . . . '

A nurse came and touched her arm. Graham Blyth was already on his feet, and together they went through to see their son.

Linda sighed and fetched herself

242

some coffee from the vending machine. Waiting was always the worst part.

She had drunk every drop by the time Richard returned, looking drained.

'How is she?' she asked gently.

'It's not that bad, although she's being kept under observation in case of internal injuries. She's got a broken wrist and a lot of abrasions. Shock.' He sighed. 'Why do we have to be built like egg-shells?'

He looked so shattered. She put her hand on his arm.

'Let me take you home, Richard. You can contact Karen's mother in the morning . . .'

★ ★ ★

'Is Nicola all right?' Fraser asked his mother when she reached his bedside.

'It wasn't Nicola who was on the bike with you, Fraser. It was Karen Mason.'

'Oh . . . yes,' he murmured before he drifted into unconsciousness again.

'Come back in the morning,' the

nurse advised. 'Perhaps he'll be more alert then.'

'Will he be all right?'

'I think so. We'll keep an eye on him in case anything develops . . . but I think it's just concussion, and his ankle and the dislocated shoulder.' She shook her head and remarked ruefully, 'Yet the driver of the car that hit them didn't have a scratch on him.'

'Maybe it wasn't the boy's fault,' Fraser's father said hopefully, looking down at his son's pale face.

Fraser had been only briefly aware of his parents' presence. Poor old Dad, he thought hazily. What a disappointment I've been to him. And now this . . .

Drifting off again, he could see The Rose, the old inn that Nicola's gran had been trying to save. Bless Mrs Moretti! She was great fun. He could see some of her character in Nicky . . .

In this trance, between waking and sleeping, Fraser found himself in the middle of a surreal dance. He was surrounded by dancing buildings. Roofs, steep or flat; columns of all kinds; doors and windows, steps and lintels.

They seemed to be smiling at him. It was the weirdest thing he'd ever seen. He half knew he was asleep and dreaming, but these mind pictures looked so real . . .

He didn't seem to be in any pain. When he drifted far enough into consciousness to know he was in hospital, he wasn't worried. His head was strangely clear. And he kept remembering those buildings.

He thought briefly about Nicky, then remembered that she wasn't here. He would remember why when he woke up, he was sure . . .

★   ★   ★

'They were on a roundabout when they were hit,' Richard said as Linda drove out of the car park. 'Thrown on to their right sides. But Fraser's concussion is the worst of it, thank goodness. I expect Karen's mother will criticise me for not taking better care of her. I should never have allowed her to . . . '

'Richard, we can't keep them prisoners. Look what I've just been through with Nicola.'

'I know what you mean. It's just so awful being a single father with a daughter . . . '

'Well, I never planned to be a single parent either,' she informed him in mock outrage, and at last he relaxed back in his seat.

Linda breathed a sigh of relief. It was good to feel him unwinding a bit.

'It's almost breakfast time,' he said as she drew up at his door. 'Come in and have coffee with me at least.'

His face looked haggard. His serious eyes, with that look which always melted her heart, were deeply shadowed. A lock of hair flopped on to his brow and, for the first time, she noticed some silver at his temples.

'Not this time. You should try to get some sleep.' She was pleased that she managed to sound matter-of-fact. 'But first you ought to phone Karen's mother — she'll want to see her.'

'Mm.' He held her gaze. 'Linda, I think you and I ought to get together.'

He put his arm round her shoulders and drew her to him, his lips descending possessively on hers.

'Marry me, Linda,' he said when they drew apart.

'Are you sure it's me you want, Richard, and not just a mother for Karen? And talking of Karen . . . how do you know she would accept me?'

'Oh, stop producing red herrings and answer me! Will you marry me?'

'I can't think straight right now, Richard, and neither can you. Please get some sleep. I'll carry on at the office till you arrive tomorrow . . . I mean today. And I'd like to visit Karen later.'

'Don't think I'm going to forget about this,' he said softly. 'I'll ask you again, and keep on asking, because we're right for each other, and you know it.' He leaned forward and kissed her forehead. 'See you later.'

Then she was staring at his closed front door, with her heart in turmoil and her head in a whirl.

★ ★ ★

That afternoon Linda found Karen lying disconsolately on top of the hospital bed, her arm in plaster and her pretty face disfigured by bruising.

'Hello, Karen.' Linda's heart twisted. No wonder Richard had been so upset! 'How are you feeling?'

'I could cry, to be honest with you,' Karen muttered.

'Cry all you want, dear. It'll do you good. But bear in mind that the bruising will soon go down and at least you've no injuries that might leave a scar.'

'Oh, you're thinking about my face? It's not that.' She shook her head. 'I'm cheesed off that my writing hand's out of commission.' She frowned. 'Still, I'm better off than Fraser. He's come round, but they're keeping him in for a bit longer . . . '

Linda put the things she'd brought on top of the locker and smiled at the girl.

'You'll be able to get about really soon, I'm sure. It's just your wrist. Bones take a little longer to heal. But I thought you might be worried about your job, so how about this?' She produced a small machine from her handbag. 'Could you carry this small tape-recorder about with you? Then I could type your notes up for you if that would be any help.'

'Linda!' Karen squealed. 'Would you? That would mean I could keep the job at the Herald. D'you promise?'

'I promise,' Linda assured her, satisfied to see the light back in the girl's eyes.

'Great! I'll get up now that there's something to get up for.' She sat up cautiously. 'Could you possibly ask Dad to bring me some clothes, please?'

'Of course. You'll have them tonight.'

By the time Linda came to go, she

felt she and Karen had become friends.

'Thanks for everything,' Karen smiled, but then Linda saw her eyes widen as she gazed past her.

'Oh, no,' Karen muttered. 'That's all I need!'

An immaculately-dressed woman swept past Linda in a cloud of discreet perfume to cast a shower of flowers and chocolates on the bed.

'Hello, Mum,' Karen said without enthusiasm. 'Mum, this is Linda Gray, Dad's secretary — Linda, my mother, Janette Black.'

So this slim, sophisticated creature was Richard's ex-wife!

Linda was appalled at the feelings that rose in her but she forced herself to murmur a conventional, 'How do you do?'

However, Janette Black wasted little time on her.

'Darling!' After one appalled look at her daughter's face, Janette smothered Karen in an embrace — under which she stiffened.

'I can see I'll have to come back home and be a proper mother to you again!' Janette was scolding as Linda left the ward.

At home, Linda stared at herself in the mirror, only too aware of the painful contrast between herself and Janette Black. Janette Black was positively glamorous by comparison. Her new husband obviously had money.

And what was that about 'coming back home' to take care of Karen? That must have been said purely for effect. And yet when she'd said it, Linda had felt a cold shock.

When Richard had proposed to her early that morning, she hadn't been at all sure she was ready to make that kind of commitment again. But now, having met the woman he had once loved, she was filled with a different kind of doubt — about herself. How could he genuinely want her — after Janette?

There was just one thing Janette had, all unwittingly, proved to her this morning. Linda wanted Richard. Right this minute she was longing for his comforting presence.

She lifted the phone and dialled his number. As she waited, she could see his smiling eyes . . .

★ ★ ★

It seemed to Nicola, still at the Ranieri villa, as if she was never alone. Angelo's friend Teresa, the private detective, was living in the house and accompanying her and Carlo everywhere.

Angelo was spending so much time there that he was hardly ever at his flat. And whenever he returned to the house in the evenings, Teresa always seemed to be in the hall, waiting to confer with him.

Teresa wasn't simply a bodyguard. She went wherever Nicola and Carlo went to spot faces in the crowd.

She looked like one of Nicola's friends, dressing like her in shorts and sun-tops or jeans and T-shirts, her tawny hair softly flowing.

Nicola's own hair was looking better than it had when she had taken the scissors to it. Angelo had personally driven her to a good hairdresser in Sorrento the following day.

'There's no need for you to drive me, Angelo,' she had protested.

'I promised your mother I wouldn't let you out of my sight — so expect to see me in your mirror!'

Secretly she was glad to be escorted. She was still shaky, and she felt safe with Angelo. For some reason she wanted to ask his advice about everything she did. She had to be stern with herself for longing to cling to him.

She hoped it wasn't jealousy she felt when she saw Teresa in those long conferences with him. The wrench of having to leave Carlo at the end of the summer was going to be terrible enough, without any added pain because of Angelo.

That night, at dinner, Giorgio admired her appearance. He said the hairstyle was much more sophisticated, and Nicola had to agree. Slowly, her confidence was beginning to blossom again.

Giorgio seemed to have lost the restlessness he had shown just after Linda had left. He was beginning to relax, and take up his old routine, going out to dine with friends or entertaining at the villa.

Angelo, Nicola and Teresa always formed part of his dinner parties, though they invariably excused themselves long before his guests left.

On one of these occasions, Nicola escaped to her favourite spot at the foot of the garden where, through the screen of vegetation, she could glimpse the sea.

Angelo silently materialised beside her, just as he had the first time they'd met here.

'Angelo! Don't creep up on me like that — it frightens me!'

'I'm sorry.' He put a hand on her shoulder. 'But I wanted to talk to you. Nicola, do you want . . . ? It strikes me we're being cruel, keeping you here because Carlo needs you. Do you want to go home?'

Her reaction to that shocked her. She didn't want to go home. Ever.

He saw how shaken she was and led her over to the garden bench.

'I know you have to finish your studies, Nicola. One more year, yes? And your mother must be longing to have you back home where she can care for you.'

But she suddenly knew with certainty that this was to be her home . . . not England.

She gazed out at the sea, breathed in the scent of the flowers, all the time conscious of Angelo at her side, patient, waiting.

'I won't leave just yet,' she hedged. 'It's too soon to leave Carlo . . . And I want to see my great-uncle Paolo, and Marta, before I go.' She looked up at him. 'It's so odd, Angelo. Every time I'm with Paolo it's as if I had Grandpa back in a way. He — smells the same! Do you know what I mean?'

He smiled at her and gave her a little hug.

'I'll drive you up to see them on Sunday. Shall we take Carlo?'

'Of course. Marta adores him.'

'Teresa can have Sunday off, so I'll be your bodyguard. Then I must start advertising for a new nanny for Carlo.'

Nicola felt a steel blade turning in her heart.

Time To Go Home . . .

It was a fortnight later. Looking around the people gathered in her sitting-room, Linda felt a little surge of happiness. It was lovely to have them all there. Gwen and Rodney, about to leave on their holiday; Gail and Steve, with the children; Karen and Richard.

Karen, with Emma on her lap, was showing her the exercises to strengthen her wrist now that the plaster was off, and Emma was trying to mimic them.

Linda had noticed that Richard was one of those people to whom animals and children gravitate, and Christopher had gone to him the instant he'd sat down to show him his drawing of a motor-bike.

He was wide-eyed and enchanted at Richard's skill with a pencil as he drew another fantasy motor-bike.

Gail, watching them together, was feeling calmer than she had felt all summer. Christopher's holidays were almost over and, surprisingly, he was looking forward to going back to school. He was an active child, who needed lots of stimulus.

She didn't think the children had noticed that they hadn't had a proper holiday this year. Steve had been good, taking Christopher fishing and giving him plenty of attention.

Steve himself had become a lot more philosophical about things. And she knew whatever happened, there would always be the two of them and they would manage.

Money wasn't everything, she thought, as she sent a smile of infinite sweetness across to her husband.

They left just before the children's bedtime, taking Karen with them as she wanted a lift to Fraser's house.

Gwen hadn't sounded surprised to hear that Karen had been visiting him so often. And she had been positively overjoyed when Karen had told them Fraser's news.

'He's going back to college.' Her eyes were shining. 'His dad's dead chuffed about it. He's decided to go for architecture after all, but he won't tell me why.'

The room seemed quiet once the youngsters were away.

'We're off the day after tomorrow to Scotland,' Rodney announced. 'Stopping to visit the Border towns first.'

'I've never seen the Border abbeys,' Gwen confided.

'Well, now you shall,' Rodney declared indulgently. 'And Linda can stop worrying about you for a fortnight.'

Linda smiled. 'All I ask is that you don't introduce her to any more ruins that have to be saved!'

'That reminds me.' Gwen sat up suddenly. 'Did you know there's talk of that beautiful path that runs along behind the mill being closed? We can't let that happen!'

The others let out a concerted groan.

'Take her on holiday, Rodney, please,' Linda begged.

After waving them off, Linda watched as they walked away, both straight-backed and gallant, towards Rodney's car.

'Your mother is so elegant,' Richard's voice said beside her.

'Isn't she? Slim and elegant. If only I'd inherited some of it!'

She glanced down at her rose-coloured jersey dress, wishing she had her mother's flair.

'The apple doesn't fall far from the tree!' Richard smiled at her. 'It's been a very pleasant evening, Linda. I love your family. Especially Emma and Christopher. He's very bright, isn't he?'

'Yes, I'm lucky that they're so lovely, and that they live nearby where I can see lots of them.'

But suddenly she knew that there was a terrible emptiness in her life.

Perhaps some of it showed in her eyes, because he paused as he was putting his jacket on.

'Don't you ever feel lonely, Linda? I'm afraid I do.'

'Of course I do. Anyone living alone is bound to now and then.'

She found it hard to keep meeting his eyes. Karen, earlier on, had mentioned in passing that her mother had dropped in a few times since she'd left hospital. Knowing that made Linda reluctant . . .

'Linda . . . ' He came closer. 'Won't you give me an answer to that question I asked you the night of Karen's accident?'

'I can't. You see — ' She had to say it. ' — I have the feeling that Janette isn't entirely out of your life.'

'What? What on earth makes you say that?'

'It was something she said at the hospital. And . . . well, she's so gorgeous that you must . . . '

He took her hands firmly in his.

'Don't be an idiot! If only you knew, Linda — ' He stopped and began to laugh. 'Sweetheart, I've had more than enough of Janette to last me several lifetimes. Believe me, I don't want Janette — I only want you.

'If you could just have seen yourself tonight, Linda. You look so lovely in that dress. And all the family there — you're so loved, so appreciated. It's you I want, you I need, my darling. You, and only you!'

He drew her into his arms, and all her doubts melted.

'Darling, I know you're not sure yet, and I don't mind waiting — for just as long as it takes you to decide that you're ready. But please don't make it too long . . .'

His lips came down crushingly, demandingly, on hers.

★ ★ ★

At the vineyard in the hills, Angelo was touched by his son's reunion with the Morettis. To his surprise, Carlo let Marta gather him into her arms, and

262

returned her bearlike hug with enthusiasm.

Nicola was embraced and kissed fondly, and he could see the truth of what she had told him about her great-uncle in the way she and Paolo were with each other.

Marta hurried to dispense coffee and amaretto biscuits, and they sat in the shade, talking.

'And soon now you have to go home?' Paolo turned to Nicola, sadness in his smile. 'I wish we could keep you here. You are like one of us!'

Once again that stab of regret pierced Nicola.

'I was only here for the summer,' she explained earnestly. 'I'm a student, I have to finish my course . . . ' She looked at Angelo, appealing for understanding.

Carlo wasn't listening. He had found the book of animals he liked and was engrossed in it.

She was afraid the little boy hadn't grasped the fact that they were about to be parted. He still clung to her a great deal, and had reverted to some of his baby ways.

How can I leave him? she wondered in despair, aware of Angelo's eyes on her.

'Of course — I understand,' Paolo said. 'But when you come back you must bring Gwen. Marco's Gwen.'

'I will,' Nicola promised. 'Oh, *Tio Paolo*, I'll never forget the miracle of your finding us that morning!'

Her great-uncle hugged her, smiling.

'I was waiting all my life to find you there!'

'You have someone else coming to look after the boy?' Marta asked anxiously, placing a coffee cup in front of Angelo. 'You must be very careful who you get.'

'Yes, I know.' Angelo's glance slipped back to Nicola. 'However, I have some news. I'll be with Carlo more myself. I'm leaving the carabinieri and taking up my place in the family business.'

Nicola's eyes were full of sympathy.

'But you love your job, Angelo! Won't you miss it?'

'Of course. But there are other things I shan't miss, and things I won't have to do again — like putting my family in danger.'

His eyes rested on his little son's dark, curly head. The look was like a caress.

'Of course the family must come first,' Marta said with finality. 'But you'll still need someone to look after Carlo?'

'Yes, I will. In fact, Signora Moretti, I wondered if you know of anyone?'

'I might,' she said slowly. 'Nicola, when do you leave?'

'Next week.'

Marta nodded, then turned back to Angelo.

'If you have not made an arrangement by then, signore, come and see me. I have a daughter, you know, Rosina . . .'

'Call me Angelo, please. And thank you. It would be good to think Nicola's cousin might want to work with Carlo.'

They smiled at each other.

'And you, cara.' Paolo turned to Nicola. 'Are you over the shock yet?'

'I don't think so. Not quite,' Nicola confessed. 'I still dream I'm in that dreadful attic — that it's on fire and I can't get us out in time . . . I wake up in a state.'

Paolo put a comforting arm around her and walked her away.

Seeing Angelo's face as his eyes followed the girl, Marta touched his arm.

'They're young and strong. They will get over it in time.'

Carlo caught sight of Paolo's dog and pointed: 'Bruno!'

Marta took his hand, leading him across to talk to him.

'And then, when I marry again, my wife will look after Carlo very carefully,' Angelo was saying.

'You are to marry again?' Paolo sounded delighted. 'It is a good thing, a young man like you!'

266

However, Angelo's words had sent Nicola's heart plummeting to the pit of her stomach.

It must be Teresa he meant.

How could she ever have been such a fool as to let herself imagine anything else? He wouldn't be letting her go home if he felt anything for her, would he?

She must keep her feelings from him — she still had some pride. There was only a week left . . . surely she could do that for a week?

★ ★ ★

The night before she was due to leave, she walked down to the belvedere to say goodbye to the beautiful coast she loved.

She leaned on the parapet, staring out at the moon-drenched sea, hoping that Angelo, deep in conversation with Teresa as usual, hadn't noticed her departure.

Fighting back the threatening tears,

she shut her eyes against the thought of separation from Carlo, from Angelo . . . The future without them was too bleak to be contemplated.

Then she felt a breath of air, and his aftershave reached her, and Angelo was beside her, gazing at the moonlit path that stretched to Capri.

'Where will you be this day next week?' he said at last.

'Re-enrolling at college.'

'Oh, yes. You must finish your degree. Then what will you do?'

'Something with my languages. Secretary for an international firm, perhaps.'

'Or you could work for an Italian firm using your English?'

'I might.' She could come back to Italy and look for a job — but how could she? This was Angelo's country, and if Teresa . . .

'I would like to know you better, Nicola.' He brushed the hair back from her forehead. 'I am sorry you are going to leave us.'

She couldn't speak.

'I never thought this English girl would turn out to be . . . well, what you have turned out to be!'

'I'm sorry to be leaving Carlo,' she managed to say evenly. She had never felt so desolate in her life. 'I've tried to say goodbye to him but I don't think he understood. I'm worried he may be upset tomorrow.'

'Oh, Teresa will cope. It's lucky she's been here all these weeks and he has grown used to her.'

'And when you marry — everything will be all right.'

'Yes.'

She struggled with rising tears until they spilled over and she was convulsed with sobs.

'You're so sorry to leave?' He gathered her into his arms as though comforting a child.

'Yes,' she gasped. 'So sorry . . . '

She tore herself out of the haven of his arms and fled.

★ ★ ★

Next morning, blinking in the early light, Nicola followed Raimondo down the stairs for the last time. He loaded her luggage into the little car, and Nicola turned to see a sleepy Carlo, held by Giorgio, holding out his arms to her.

''Bye, darling.' She hugged him fiercely, so tightly that he protested. But Giorgio was firm with him.

'Be good, Carlo, and let Nicola catch her plane. When she is home with her mother she may phone you.'

'Would you like that, Carlo?' She kissed him again. 'Goodbye, angel.'

He was dangling the toy she had given him, a cuddly dog that somehow looked like Bruno.

The streets and buildings were still drained of colour as Angelo drove her through the town. The airport had a swept look before the bustle of the day built up. A few tourist buses arrived, the returning holiday-makers yawning.

Once Nicola had checked in, they stood together in the terminal.

'Well, goodbye, Angelo!' She turned to shake hands with him.

He looked intently into her eyes, and she prayed that he couldn't read there her intense longing. Then she turned away and joined the queue straggling towards the gate.

Safely away from him, she brought out her handkerchief and mopped her eyes.

There was a little delay, and then he was there again, standing a few feet away from her, motionless, his heart in his eyes.

He opened his arms. 'Nicola!'

Incredulous, she turned and took a step towards him, irresistibly drawn.

'*Cara mia.*' His voice was husky as he gathered her into his arms. 'I love you.'

She drew away and looked up at him. She couldn't believe it. But the love was plain to see, shining in his eyes.

'I know you must go home now, *cara*, but as soon as we can, Carlo and I will come over to see you. Certainly for Christmas, yes?'

'Oh, Angelo!' She was swept away by his first kiss.

'This is crazy,' she said shakily. 'I just want to stay.'

'No. You must go.' He kissed her again. 'You have to finish your degree. You have friends to see, family, yes? But next summer, when your course is over, you will come back to me, and to Carlo, for good. Then, Nicky, you will be my wife.'

As the plane took off, Nicola gazed towards the terminal. She couldn't see him, didn't know where he was standing. But somewhere in that building was the man who held her heart, and their future, in his hands . . .

THE END

We do hope that you have enjoyed reading this large print book.

Did you know that all of our titles are available for purchase?

We publish a wide range of high quality large print books including:
Romances, Mysteries, Classics
General Fiction
Non Fiction and Westerns

Special interest titles available in large print are:
The Little Oxford Dictionary
Music Book, Song Book
Hymn Book, Service Book

Also available from us courtesy of Oxford University Press:
Young Readers' Dictionary
(large print edition)
Young Readers' Thesaurus
(large print edition)

For further information or a free brochure, please contact us at:
Ulverscroft Large Print Books Ltd.,
The Green, Bradgate Road, Anstey,
Leicester, LE7 7FU, England.
Tel: (00 44) 0116 236 4325
Fax: (00 44) 0116 234 0205

Other titles in the
Linford Romance Library:

THREE TALL TAMARISKS

Christine Briscomb

Joanna Baxter flies from Sydney to run her parents' small farm in the Adelaide Hills while they recover from a road accident. But after crossing swords with Riley Kemp, life is anything but uneventful. Gradually she discovers that Riley's passionate nature and quirky sense of humour are capturing her emotions, but a magical day spent with him on the coast comes to an abrupt end when the elegant Greta intervenes. Did Riley love Greta after all?